[illegible]TE OAKS

Judy's husb[illegible] Gordon, wants a change. After years at [illegible]e's ready to come ashore. A seaside gues[illegible]us really floats his boat and Judy, suppo[illegible]ve [illegible]s ever, goes with the flow. Then he's ca[illegible] away leaving Judy to renovate the house[illegible]nd staff and run a business she never [illegible]nted. Add to the mix parents from hell, [illegible]mitten neighbour and a daughter with a [illegible]ller coaster love and you have to wonder [illegible]udy will pull it off. And what will hap[illegible] when Gordon comes home again?

WHITE OAKS

WHITE OAKS

by

Lyn McCulloch

Dales Large Print Books
Long Preston, North Yorkshire,
BD23 4ND, England.

British Library Cataloguing in Publication Data.

McCulloch, Lyn
White Oaks.

A catalogue record of this book is
available from the British Library

ISBN 978-1-84262-672-6 pbk

Published in Large Print 2009 by arrangement with
Lyn McCulloch

Dales Large Print is an imprint of Library Magna Books Ltd.

Printed and bound in Great Britain by
T.J. (International) Ltd., Cornwall, PL28 8RW

One

Leaving it all Behind

'It's ours!' Gordon put down the phone and hugged her, smearing the butter from her toast all around her mouth. 'We've exchanged contracts.' He tried to polka round the kitchen but she was off-balance and they ended up in a tangled heap against the freezer.

Judy leant breathlessly against the cold door, as he stood over her, his hands either side of her shoulders. Bosun, a small wiry Jack Russell terrier, took up the polka and danced round them barking frantically.

'Shut up, dog!' they cried in unison.

Gordon's eyes sparkled with excitement. 'We, you and me, are going to be the proud owners of White Oaks Guest House in Sandhaven!' She tried to summon up the right degree of eagerness. 'This is the beginning of a whole new life, Jude.'

She couldn't answer. Fortunately, he took her silence as shortness of breath rather than lack of enthusiasm.

He released her and she wiped the butter from her face and reached for her coffee as he turned to the sink to start washing up.

No way out then. This is it.

Gordon began to sing 'The best is yet to come' and she pulled herself together.

She'd agreed to this move so she might as well try to share his anticipation. She chimed in with him, 'The best is yet to come and babe, won't that be fine? You think you've seen the sun, but you ain't seen it shine!' He grinned at her as he reached for the tea towel.

'Five short weeks, babe! Sandhaven here we come!'

'Don't cry, just don't cry!' Judy clenched her teeth to keep the smile in place and looked out across the sea of faces in the school hall.

'I've loved my years at Barn Road,' she assured teachers and pupils alike, but was saved from further embarrassment by Jack from Year Six.

'You going to open the present, Miss?' he called from the back and the pupils took up the refrain.

'Yes, go on, Miss, open it!'

'I'll do it, Miss!'

Judy's hands were shaking and she wasn't sure she could cope with the elaborate ribbons round the gift, undoubtedly wrapped by Miss Watson, the Art Teacher. She looked down at the front row, bright-eyed and keen, sitting cross-legged staring up at her.

'Brandon,' she picked the youngster who'd spent most time in her office with grazed knees and other playground injuries. Life as a school secretary had never been dull. 'Would you like to help me open my present?'

Brandon nodded eagerly.

'Come on then.'

Brandon clambered up onto the stage and with one almighty yank, pulled the package from the paper, tearing it and leaving the ribbons in a heap round his feet. 'There you are, Miss.' He handed her a small flat box from a very expensive London jeweller, together with an envelope.

Judy's tears began to fall as she grinned. 'That wasn't quite what I had in mind but thanks anyway.' She looked at the box. What on earth could it be?

Brandon stood his ground, looking up at her. 'What is it, Miss?'

She glanced across at the head teacher who gave an encouraging nod.

Inside the box, lying on a bed of scarlet

crushed velvet was a gold-plated egg timer. Judy burst out laughing. 'That's a really useful present!' She held it up for all to see.

'What's it for, Miss?' Brandon looked disappointed.

The whole ceremony took on a slightly surreal quality as she realised that few of the children had a clue what an egg timer was and she was therefore compelled to explain the principles of cooking perfectly boiled eggs.

When she'd finished, the head stood and smiled. 'We wanted to give you something appropriate and it was hard to find anything. It came from a catalogue entitled "For the woman who has everything."'

'As if...!'

'Well, in the envelope is something that might be more practical.'

From the envelope, Judy pulled a card, with what looked like a million signatures on it. She knew she didn't dare look at those yet. They would definitely provoke tears. There was also a very generous cheque.

'Wow! Too much!' she was overcome. 'Thank you all so much!'

'It was just going to be a collection from the staff, but so many parents asked to be involved that it grew like Topsy. Hope you'll find it useful anyhow.'

'I think it may just save us from starvation in the first few weeks,' Judy quipped, though there was a hint of panic-stricken honesty in her voice.

Judy was left alone on the stage as the children filed out of the hall. The staff gathered round to wish her well.

'Come and stay,' she pleaded. 'Do come! I'm going to need all the friendly faces I can get.'

'Try keeping us away,' Miss Watson, the Art teacher grinned. 'My boyfriend's already planning a weekend in Sandhaven in the summer.'

'Oh,' Judy suddenly blushed, embarrassed, 'the only thing is … well, you have to pay. I feel awful after this,' she brandished the cheque, 'but we're not going to be able to afford any freebies.'

'Don't be daft,' the head interrupted quickly. 'No one expects that.' But judging from the look on one or two faces, Judy was not so sure.

Half an hour later she lay back in the passenger seat of the car. She'd arranged for Gordon to pick her up so that she could have a farewell glass of bubbly with the staff. 'Whew!'

He was concentrating on negotiating the school gates. 'Okay?'

She gave a watery grin. 'Yes, look!'

She produced the egg timer from her handbag with a flourish and he laughed. 'I bought a digital one from the pound shop the other day but it'll add a bit of class to the kitchen.'

For a moment, she wondered whether to show him the cheque. If it came to it, there was a bit of a nest egg there to feed them for a few weeks if things went really wrong.

'Just an egg timer? That's a bit tight after all your years of loyal service.'

She relented, unable to bear him thinking badly of her generous colleagues and parents. 'No, there was this as well.' She showed him the cheque and he whistled appreciatively.

'That'll come in handy. Buy a few bedspreads or something.'

She tested the water. 'I thought I might keep it for a treat. A spa day or something with Jan when I really need it.'

He laughed. 'Why would you want to do that. Every day's going to feel like a holiday when we get to Sandhaven!'

Judy took a last look at the sitting room,

stripped of furniture and all the little personal touches, pale squares where pictures used to be and scuff marks that didn't show when a place was lived in.

'It's only four walls,' Gordon had said, 'Once all our stuff's gone it's a house, not a home.' Deep down she knew he was right, but it still hurt. She heard the car start outside.

The front door closed with a decisive click and she pushed it to make quite sure it was locked. Gordon had already delivered the keys to the agent so there was no going back in. Probably for the best.

There was a cry from the end of the cul de sac. 'Hang on!' Jan was running towards her, a parcel in her hand. 'I nearly forgot I'd got this for you,' she thrust the parcel at Judy. 'Don't open it till you get there.'

Gordon tooted the horn impatiently and called her from the car window. 'Jude, we've got to go. The removal men will be there ahead of us if we don't get a move on.'

'I can't believe we're really going.' Judy whispered, wrapping Jan in a bear hug. 'Come down and see me really, really soon.'

'Of course I will and you ring me tonight and let me know you're all right.'

'I will.' Judy dabbed her eyes, hoping her

contact lenses had survived the sudden flood, and climbed into the passenger seat beside Gordon. She wound down the window and waved as they drove down Laurel Drive and round the corner, away from the life she knew, understood and loved.

As they headed towards the motorway, Judy was quiet. Gordon glanced across at her as he negotiated the roundabout and joined the ring road. 'Regrets?'

'No, of course not,' she lied, 'just thinking about Jan. It's going to seem odd without her.' Judy secretly suspected that Gordon was quite pleased to get her away from her best friend. Sometimes she wondered if he was jealous of their closeness. 'Don't worry about me, I'm just being silly.'

Gordon squeezed her hand. 'This is for us, you and me. Time to move on, love.'

'I know, but who do I call when something goes wrong? It's always been Jan.' It was true. Their children had all grown up together and Jan and Martin were like second parents to Lucy and Tom. When Gordon was at sea and a problem arose that needed male input – plumbing, things to go in the loft, catching and evicting spiders – Jan would send Martin round. One thing would lead to another and the day usually ended with a meal in one or other of the houses or a barbecue if the weather was right.

'I'll be there,' Gordon reassured her.

She smiled uncertainly.

When he had suggested they buy a seaside guest house she'd scoffed at the idea, thinking he was joking but the more they'd talked about it the more she understood that it made sense. Gordon couldn't stay at sea forever, and there was little call for Merchant Navy Navigating Officers in Middle England. He was too young to retire properly and so the idea of buying a business had grown.

The children were doing their own thing now. Tom, in his second year at University, had made it clear that he had no intention of ever living at home again. Lucy was sharing a flat in London with the ghastly Jason and showed no sign of seeing sense and leaving him. Even if she did, her job in Exhibition Management meant that she had to remain city-based. So, they really didn't need to consider the offspring, Gordon wanted to come ashore, but he needed to earn. This was an ideal solution.

Judy's job as a school secretary hadn't even entered into the equation. Gordon had only ever treated it as something she did to keep herself amused while he was away and it had, of course, been very convenient when the children were at school. He had just assumed she would give it up without any qualms and he'd been genuinely surprised when he realised how much it mattered to her.

'I've been there fifteen years,' she'd explained, 'I'm part of the furniture now. There's so much I do that isn't even documented. It just happens.'

He'd been brusque. 'No-one's indispensable. They'll manage without you. In fact, it'll do them good. They'll really appreciate you when you're gone.' Judy wasn't too sure of the logic of that one, but she'd let it go and had also refrained from pointing out that her salary had contributed a significant amount to the family budget and was, in fact, still paying Tom's University tuition fees and rent.

The car purred relentlessly towards the South coast and Judy closed her eyes. There wouldn't be much opportunity for sleep in the next few weeks; perhaps an hour or so of oblivion would help her see all this as an adventure.

Two

In at the Deep End

Judy gasped as they rounded the bend and Gordon slowed the car so that they could fully appreciate Sandhaven Bay spread out ahead of them. It was perfect. The sea sparkled, there were yachts scattered at anchor and the sun shone from a clear blue sky.

Gordon grinned. 'It is pretty spectacular, isn't it?'

She nodded. 'I suppose one day we won't even notice it. But it feels like the kind of place you come to on holiday. I can't believe we're really going to live here.'

'Well, you'd better get used to it. We'll be quite blasé about this view in no time.'

Judy picked up the estate agent's details from the dashboard. They were crumpled from being re-read and passed round to friends, all incredulous at this sudden move. 'Do you think we can find it without getting lost this time?'

'It's this one way system, it's really confusing.'

'Yeah, yeah. Call yourself a navigator?'

'I do that on water. It's easy at sea, you just do it by the sun and stars.'

'Look for the Italian restaurant. That's the landmark we need.'

'It'll be handy having that at the bottom of the hill. For when we don't have time to cook.'

'We can't afford to eat out for a while. There's an awful lot to do.' Judy paused. 'It's all a bit scary, isn't it? Aren't you just a tiny bit nervous? What if we can't do it?'

Gordon squeezed her hand and she began to feel just a little smidgen of hope and excitement. 'It'll be fine.'

A barrage of barking erupted from the back seat as Bosun, who thought he was the biggest dog in the world, spotted a Dalmatian walking blamelessly beside the sea.

They both laughed. 'Bosun, it doesn't all belong to you!' The dog presented yet another problem. 'Do you think he'll ever let a guest into White Oaks?'

'He'll add character.' Gordon gave a reassuring smile. 'Look, there's the Italian.' There was a pretty little trattoria on the left and Gordon swung the car up the steep hill opposite before drawing up outside an Edwardian building that had clearly seen better days. They sat in the car and surveyed their new home. The printed details called it 'charming but dilapidated'. It was an attractive house with a wrought iron balcony and original sash windows. In estate-agent-speak it had potential, but as far as Judy could see it was simply in need of an awful lot of work.

'Oh, well,' Judy took a deep breath. 'Let's do it.' She turned to the dog in the back. 'You can stay there for now. You're in the shade.'

A sharp-suited young man stood in the porch. He greeted them, right hand outstretched.

'Hi there, today's the day then!' The estate agent grabbed Gordon's hand and shook it forcefully, while waving a set of keys in her face. 'Here we are!' He paused for effect and then presented the keys with a big flourish. For an awful moment Judy wondered if he might be about to carry her over the threshold but Gordon thanked him and dismissed him firmly, promising coffee any time he was passing.

They let themselves in.

Judy looked around the dingy hall. It was

painted a lurid shade of pink with a truly dreadful 1950's carpet on the floor. She blinked at the multi-coloured swirls; this had to be one of the first changes. 'How long do you think we have till the vans arrive?'

'Oh, at least an hour or so.' Gordon threw open the door to the dining room, which looked as though breakfast was just about to take place. The previous owners had promised to leave everything ready. Each table was laid up with rose-covered crockery that just shouted 'guest house', but unfortunately the cloths underneath were stained.

'Come on, let's do a quick tour of inspection. Find out what we've really let ourselves in for.'

The house was on three floors with bedrooms coming off each half landing. There was a mix of single, double and family rooms and the estate agent's particulars said that when completely full the place could sleep thirty. Breakfast for thirty? Now that was a daunting thought.

'We'll start at the top.' Gordon bounded up the stairs and Judy followed more sedately.

'These stairs will take a bit of getting used to,' she puffed as they reached the top landing.

The attic rooms could be quite pretty with their sloping ceilings and lovely sea views. The effect was spoilt, though, by the overwhelming musty smell and the pink flowery wallpaper peeling at every seam. Judy felt a wall. It was damp to the touch. 'It's soaking up here. The roof must be leaking!' She was horrified.

'Probably just a loose tile or damp leaching through the old bricks. I'll make it a priority.' Gordon's optimism was reassuring, but she began to feel it might be downright unrealistic.

'But, Gordon, we can't let rooms like this.'

'They did!' It was true. The previous owners had been trading until the day they left, so the rooms must have been in use. Judy, though, knew she couldn't bring herself to show anyone into them. She'd be too embarrassed.

They worked their way downstairs, propping open doors to let the air circulate as they went. The lower floors were better. The rooms were shabby and far from clean, but after a good scrub they would be useable until they could put their own stamp on them.

The bathrooms needed serious attention, though. No amount of cleaning could improve them. The black mould, caused, no doubt, by years of damp and lack of care, was very obvious, the grouting had seen better days and in some rooms there were bizarre colour combinations: orange shower cubicles cohabited with avocado wash basins and mint green lavatories. It could have been an attempt at 'seventies psychedelia or, more probably, a job lot had fallen off the back of some lorry and sold off cheap. Either way, changing them had to be high on Gordon's ever-lengthening list of priorities.

She sank on to the stairs. 'We're going to need some staff, you know. This is beyond just us.'

Gordon, who seemed to be in full-on Pollyanna mode, laughed off the suggestion. 'We'll be all right. Once we get sorted out, we'll just work our way through the rooms.'

Judy felt a very small kernel of despair begin to form somewhere deep inside her. She had an awful feeling they'd taken on too much.

'We're a good team, you and me.' He broke into 'You and Me against the World' which seemed to have become his theme tune and Judy forced a smile, determined not to burst his optimistic bubble.

The letting rooms were all fully furnished; bedding and everything was included in the sale, but their own belongings were on the furniture vans, still trundling down the motorway. Judy was not sure how the contents of their four bedroom house would fit into the small flat at the back of the hotel, but that was the least of their problems and there was a big, allegedly dry, cellar for the left-overs.

Finally they reached their own quarters. All empty rooms look bleak but this took the biscuit. It was almost unbelievable that anyone could wallpaper an already dark room in navy blue and then add lilac gloss paint to complete the picture. But that's what they'd inherited and would have to live with for the foreseeable future. Even Gordon couldn't put any positive spin on that.

The doorbell rang. 'At last!' muttered Judy as she went to answer it. 'Hopefully that's the rest of our possessions!' The front door, she'd noticed before, was beautiful. The stained glass panels looked original and created a kaleidoscope as the sun streamed through. It would be glorious in the summer.

There was no sign of a removal van, but on the doorstep was a young woman with a huge bouquet. 'Mrs Harcourt?'

'Yes.'

'Here you are then. Welcome to your new home,' the girl smiled and hurried off down the path as Judy tried to hold the flowers and open the envelope attached to the cellophane at the same time.

'Who are they from?'

Judy finally broke into the envelope and grinned broadly. She handed the card to Gordon. 'Tom!' She read aloud. '"Way to go, parents!" I'll be down to see you soon. Love, Tom.'

'Way to go? What's that supposed to mean? Don't they teach these kids English any more? Told you he wouldn't be able to stay away for long.'

Their son was having the time of his life at University. He'd gone off the previous October, going straight to Bristol from school. Judy had missed him more than she'd ever imagined. He had a big personality and the house was extraordinarily quiet without him and his stuff. He'd thrown himself into University life and didn't come home much so Judy was really chuffed that he'd remembered them today and wondered if Lucy had reminded him. Organisation was not his strong point but he always came through in the end.

'I'd like one of the kids to see it at its worst.'

Gordon took the flowers from her and went to the kitchen to put them in the sink. 'It might be better if Lucy didn't see it quite like this. She won't want to get any dirt under her fingernails! Tom'll be down soon though. He's nosy!'

Judy followed him into the kitchen. She'd never been particularly domesticated, always preferring gardening to housework. The closest she'd come to catering was Evening Classes in cake decoration and she'd done a few wedding and birthday cakes for friends. However, the ability to create perfect sugar roses was going to be absolutely no help at all when it came to cooking a battalion of breakfasts.

She looked round in despair.

Circa 1974 it must have been state of the art, but the range-style cooker was filthy, the mock-wood worktops were greasy to the eye and sticky to the touch and the overall effect was one of abject squalor, and she suspected it was downright unhygienic.

She ran a finger over the worktop, screwing up her face in disgust.

He put his arm round her. 'We'll have it

cleaned up in no time.'

She was too tired and dispirited to argue but she really wondered if they'd bitten off more than they could chew and was glad to be saved from answering by another ring on the bell.

A different florist's van was outside and a harassed looking woman handed over another beautiful bouquet. 'Flowers for you,' she said unnecessarily and clumped off down the path. Judy carried the flowers back to the kitchen where Gordon relieved her of them, opening the card as he headed for the sink.

'From Lucy?' she asked.

'No, bizarrely they're from Tom too! "Good luck in your new venture. Love Tom".'

'Probably drunk when he ordered the first lot and doesn't remember doing it,' Gordon speculated as he added them to the first bouquet. 'We'd better unpack a vase or two!'

'Put the whole lot in a bucket. There's too many for a vase anyhow.'

The bell rang again and they looked at each other and laughed. 'Tell me that's not another bouquet from Tom,' Gordon chuckled as he went to answer the door, coming back with an elaborately wrapped box with a courier's label on it marked 'URGENT, FRAGILE, THREE HOUR DELIVERY'.

'Who's that from?'

'Whoever it is, they've got a lot of money and left it to the last minute.'

'Lucy!' they said together and Gordon fought his way through the packaging to reveal a bottle of Krug and a card. 'Wishing you every success in your new venture. Love Lucy and Jason.'

Judy took the champagne and put it in the fridge. 'Sussed it,' she said. 'Lucy assumes Tom won't remember and gets her secretary to order flowers from him and champagne from her, but, miraculously, Tom remembered.'

'Hey,' said Gordon. 'Well worked out. That'll be good for a wind-up later!'

'Don't be mean,' Judy warned. 'At least they both bothered.'

'True, but I'll still have some sport when I talk to Tom.'

The removal men had gone and Gordon and Judy were sprawled on the sofa, which stood in state, a little oasis among the boxes. Bosun sat staring fixedly at the remains of a take-away pizza on the coffee table. The dog whined and shifted his paws hopefully.

'No, Bosun. It's not for you. Did you feed him?'

'No, I thought you had. No wonder he's hungry.'

'I'll do it.' Judy forced herself to her feet. She was beyond exhaustion and totally overwhelmed by the work they'd taken on. She'd put the dog food in a noticeable bag so they couldn't lose it. 'Where's that pink carrier bag?'

Gordon looked around helplessly at the chaos. 'I think it must still be in the car. I'll go.'

'Don't worry. I'm up now.' Judy picked up her keys and went out to the car. The pink carrier bag had fallen behind the passenger seat and as Judy reached for it she noticed the parcel from Jan on the back seat.

After feeding the dog in the hotel kitchen, figuring that the general filth wouldn't poison him even if she wouldn't eat anything prepared in there, she took the present through to their sitting room.

Gordon had fallen asleep in the chair, mouth open, snoring gently. She sat on the sofa and undid the wrapping paper – Christmas, she noticed. Well, that was Jan but it's the thought that counts and Judy knew how much she must care to have achieved wrapping it at all.

The paper revealed a beautiful red, leather-bound Visitors Book; perfect for the hall table though Judy wasn't sure she was ready to invite comments from her guests. She opened the book to find that Jan had written the first comment: 'With hosts like Judy and Gordon, how could this fail to be the best B&B in Sandhaven!'

Overcome with tiredness and loneliness, Judy reached for her phone and punched in the number she knew so well, taking herself off to sit on the stairs so as not to wake Gordon.

'Jan, you're a total star. What a great present! It's the poshest thing in this whole place – apart from the gold egg-timer, of course!'

'So how did it go?'

'We're in, let's just say that.'

'You sound really down.'

'Not really. Just worn out. Too weary to know how I feel.'

'Too tired for gossip?'

Judy perked up immediately. It had always amazed her how Jan managed to know exactly what was happening in the entire neighbourhood without leaving the house. 'Go on!'

Jan entertained Judy with a piece of scandal about a couple in the street who appeared to have behaved badly at someone's barbecue the previous weekend. Judy still couldn't quite take in the idea that these weren't her neighbours any more. 'Anyway,' Jan concluded, 'how about you? What's it really like?'

Judy gave Jan an audio tour of the house and the condition they'd found it in.

'You're going to have your work cut out. When do you expect your first guests?'

'Two weeks.'

'I could come down for a couple of days next week with my rubber gloves and mop.'

'I'd love to see you, but you can't come down here and work. That wouldn't be fair.'

'Don't be daft. Look ring me in a couple of days and if you need me, I'll be there.'

They said their goodbyes and as Judy pressed 'end', she thought how lucky she was to have a friend like Jan. She rose from the bottom stair, stretched and looked at her watch: ten o'clock. She yawned. There was such a lot to do tomorrow that she might as well go to bed.

She thought of the children. Lucy and Jason were probably just about to go out to some sophisticated night-club and Tom would be up for hours yet, setting the world to rights with his friends at University. She felt like an old fogey as she banged the sitting room door to wake Gordon and headed for the bathroom. Thank Heavens she'd thought to make the bed soon after their furniture arrived. She couldn't have faced doing it now.

Their bathroom boasted a turquoise suite and more of the ghastly navy blue flowery wallpaper that adorned the living room, but she couldn't even begin to think what they would eventually do to their flat. Best to concentrate on the rooms that would make them money first.

Bosun was ahead of her, curled up right in the middle of the duvet, obviously hoping that if he kept his eyes shut, no one would notice he was there. Gordon joined her and looked affectionately down at the dog. 'Let him stay. He must be wondering what's going on with all the upheaval.'

Judy, too shattered to argue, crept in beside the dog and was asleep before Gordon was out of the bathroom.

Two days later, Gordon's list of priorities had reached humungous proportions. The damp in the attic rooms was an urgent problem and Gordon had finally conceded that they needed a roofer to quote for that. There was a problem with the central heating. The rooms on the top floor seemed to get very hot whilst in the ones below the radiators were barely warm and the whole house was still filthy. She knew they should have started with the kitchen, but that was just too daunting. Tomorrow, she vowed. Tomorrow, they'd get to it.

On the plus side, though, she loved Sandhaven. Everyone talked to each other. She was already greeted as an old friend in the hardware shop where she seemed to have spent quite a lot of the last couple of days getting screws, nails and hinges to help Gordon make temporary repairs to various doors, cupboards and beds that were only just hanging together. She guessed she would get used to the queues at the supermarket check-out while people discussed their latest operations, the grandchildren and other urgent topics and the way total strangers wished her a jaunty 'Good Morning' as they passed in the street was an absolute tonic.

She sat on a stool in the kitchen eating a piece of toast. It couldn't be called cosy, but the worktop where the toaster sat was no longer thick with grease. They were still only camping out; take-aways had been the best option in the evenings. Gordon came in with the post and she put some more bread in the toaster. His hair was still wet from the shower and he looked young and boyish. She smiled.

'No bills,' he flicked through the envelopes. 'That's good.'

'Anything interesting?'

'No, not from the look of it. Mostly adverts. Oh, and a letter from your mother.'

Damn! Judy was already feeling guilty about her parents. She knew she should ring them and tell them how it was all going, but she also knew that their disapproval of the whole 'madcap scheme' as they'd put it, would just depress her. She didn't need anyone telling her now that they'd known the whole move was a ridiculous plan in the first place.

She opened the letter and a five-pound note floated to the floor. 'Darling, get yourself some nice smellies with this. You mustn't let yourself go!'

Judy laughed. Her mother was just unbelievable. She looked down at her chipped nails and paint spattered jeans and was grateful that her parents were safely ensconced in London. They divided their time between a flat in Chelsea and a smart water-front development near Dartmouth. Judy needed the place in much better shape than this before she visited.

She read on. 'They want to book a room next month. They say they'll come as paying guests and pretend they don't know us.'

'No way! Tell them we're full.'

'I can't. They won't believe me.'

'Well, let's worry about them another time. Have you rung them since we've been here?'

'No, I can't face it!'

'Well, do it and tell them what it's like. Tell them we've got an outbreak of some terrible disease. They won't want to come then.'

'I'll ring them tonight and try to put them off,' Judy promised, 'now, what are your plans for today?'

'I'm going to strip all the wallpaper off the two top rooms. They're no use as they are and it'll give the walls a chance to dry out. Matt down the pub has given me the names of a couple of roofers, can you call them and try to get them round to quote?'

'Okay and then I'm going into Bournemouth to buy some sheets and towels. I just can't use the bedding that's here. The sheets are practically worn through. They're horrible.'

'Right. You'd better get some tablecloths while you're out too. The ones in the dining room are disgusting.'

'They're on the list.'

'I don't know which is longer. Your shopping list or my schedule of jobs to do.'

Judy stood up as Gordon headed for the stairs, steamer in hand. 'Doesn't matter. It's all got to be done. Give me the numbers of these roofers and then I'll go out.'

She had just grabbed her car keys when Gordon called her. 'Jude, quick!'

Throwing her keys and bag to the ground she rushed upstairs, fear making her feet fly. If Gordon had fallen off the ladder or hurt himself she didn't think she could cope. She was nearly at the end of her tether and it wouldn't take much to push her over the edge.

He was on his knees on the landing, with a floorboard up and his thumb on a pipe.

'What the…?'

'Don't ask! The floorboard was loose, so I popped a nail in it and went through the pipe. Hold it while I go and turn the water off.' She knelt beside him and replaced his thumb with hers. He stood up and rushed off down the stairs.

'Just don't let go.'

‘How long will you be?’ she called, envisaging him heading off to the plumbers’ merchant, while she knelt there like the little Dutch boy in the story.

‘I’m only going to the cellar to turn the water off, then I’ll have to drain the system.’ She shuffled to try to get comfortable, abandoning all hope of a shopping trip.

The ’phone rang and she heard Gordon answer it. She couldn’t hear what was being said, but from his tone she knew he wasn’t pleased with what he was hearing. She hoped it wasn’t Lucy bending his ear about Jason. This really wasn’t the moment. The ’phone clicked and she heard him carry on towards the cellar. It seemed ages before he came back, carrying a bucket and a length of hose. He looked terrible, his face was ashen and he looked as though he’d aged ten years.

‘Who was that on the ’phone?’

‘The office.’

‘Why do they bother you when you’re on leave. I trust you told them their fortune.’

‘Not exactly.’ He carried on up the stairs to a bathroom where she could hear him grovelling under the bath for a stopcock.

‘What did they want?’

Silence.

‘Gordon?’

'I've got to go back to sea.' His voice was muffled but the words were clear enough.

'What? When?'

Silence again.

'Gordon, when?'

'Day after tomorrow.'

Stunned, she loosened her grip on the pipe and a spurt of freezing cold water hit her straight in the face. She screamed.

'Jude?'

She shook, like Bosun after he'd been hosed down in the garden. 'I'm okay, just soaked. Now, tell me you're joking.'

There was a pause as he extricated himself from the bath and came down the stairs to her. 'Someone's been taken ill and had to be shipped home. I'm the only relief available and I'm still on contract till June. I can't say no.'

'But…' She was totally lost for words. 'You can't!' The water was dripping from her fringe into her eyes and her thumb was beginning to hurt. She could feel tears coming.

'Oh, Jude, I'm sorry.' He ruffled her hair, but she shrugged him off.

She wanted so badly to storm out of the house, get in the car and just drive, but she couldn't. She was stuck holding this damned pipe.

'I don't believe it. This is your project. Your idea! And what do you do, clear off when the going gets tough.'

'That's not fair.' It wasn't. Deep down she knew that but she didn't feel like being fair.

'How long's it going to take to drain the system?'

'Not long now. You'll manage, Jude, you know you will.'

'Actually, I don't. Good old capable Judy just might not manage this time. How on earth am I supposed to get this place ready to open on my own.'

'Jan might come down.'

'Yes. She might. Goes to show that friends are a whole lot more reliable than husbands, doesn't it.' Her tears were now mixing with the drips from her hair and she knew she made a completely pathetic picture. And she had pins and needles in her ankles from kneeling.

Gordon stepped over her and went back to his stopcock. 'Okay, you can let go,' he called and she stood up, very very slowly.

'Ouch!' her feet hurt as the blood poured back into them. 'I'm going out. I don't know when I'll be back,' she tried to head off down the stairs, but her legs wouldn't work properly and Gordon caught up with her and turned her round to give her a hug.

'It'll be fine.'

'No, Gordon, I don't think it will be fine. "Fine" is not a word I want to hear any more. I can't do this and actually I don't see why I should, either.' She felt her legs beginning to work again and turned on her heel, fuming.

'I'm leaving,' she called. 'I've got shopping to do for my business. See if you can stay long enough to hold the fort while I go to Bournemouth.' She slammed the front door so hard that the glass shook.

A hundred yards down the hill, she had to park up as she couldn't see for tears. What a mess!

Her phone rang and she ignored it. Let him stew. She knew she'd been unreasonable and when she got home she'd apologise but she was so frightened. She just didn't know if she could do this without Gordon.

Three

Home Alone

Judy waved until Gordon's taxi turned the corner. Then she sank down on to the front door step with tears streaming down her face. Her mother had drummed into her many years before that life wasn't fair, but this took the biscuit.

She knew it wasn't Gordon's fault, but the fact remained that buying White Oaks had been his idea, and now he'd gone away to sea for four months and left her on her own in a strange town with a business she knew next to nothing about.

An elderly neighbour walking past paused uncertainly. 'You all right, love?'

She forced a watery smile. 'Fine. Hay-fever, you know!' Even to her this sounded more than a little lame in the second week of February, but the old man nodded sagely and walked on swinging his shopping bag, pleased, no doubt, that this was one ailment he didn't have.

After a few minutes common sense kicked in and Judy rose, shut the door and headed for her bedroom to repair the damage the tears had done. A dab of cold water, and some make-up and a few minutes later the transformation was complete, from a sad white mouse with pink eyes to a serious businesswoman who had a job to do. And, she reminded herself, there was now only her to do it. Bosun sat in the doorway; his big brown eyes following her every move. He'd seen this before and knew the signs. His master wouldn't be back for a while.

The plan had been that they would do all the work themselves until they saw what kind of help was needed. They didn't want to employ people and then find themselves overstaffed and have to lay them off. Neither of them, they'd argued, was afraid of a bit of hard work and this was a new adventure.

So much for Gordon coming ashore for good! Gordon was on his way to Heathrow to join a ship in New Orleans while Judy was left in Sandhaven, where she noticed it had now started to rain, to run a business for which she had absolutely no experience.

A quick call to Lucy had yielded nothing. She was sorry, she would have come to the rescue but it was Jason's parents' silver wedding and she couldn't possibly miss it. Judy wondered if Gordon was right about the effect Jason had on their daughter.

She took a deep breath and sat at her desk to write a card for the newsagent's window. First things first. A chambermaid. Someone who'd come in and make beds and clean rooms. If she was going to run the place single-handed she simply couldn't do the bedrooms as well.

The phone disturbed her train of thought and she knew she sounded snappy as she answered, 'White Oaks Guest House. Can I help you?'

'Hey, you sound stressed. I'll call you back.'

Judy felt herself relax. 'Jan. Sorry. Gordon's just gone and I was trying to compose an advert for a Chambermaid.'

'That's easy. Wanted. Someone to do all the things I don't want to do.'

Judy grinned. 'Actually that's about it. You offering?'

'Not permanently, but I wondered if you'd like me to come down? I was thinking that I could leave around lunchtime and spend a couple of days. Martin's gone to Amsterdam for a meeting, so I'm kicking my heels.'

Judy knew this wasn't true. Jan was always busy, but she appreciated the tactful way she'd suggested it and she just needed to see her friend. 'Oh, yes, please. That'd be great.'

'Okay. I've got the map you left so expect me about midnight.'

'Jan, it's easy. Even you can't get lost.'

'I'm dying to see this white elephant you've taken on anyway. See you later. I'll bring some wine and we'll have a take-away tonight.'

Judy finished her cards with a triumphant flourish. Nothing seemed quite so hard now. She couldn't wait to see Jan. It was less than a week since they'd moved, but it felt like a lifetime and she could really do with a good laugh. Jan could always be relied on to put every crisis in perspective.

Ten minutes later she was in the shop at the bottom of their hill, being given the rundown on the latest goings on in the local pub where they were, apparently, considering changing from standard pub grub to a Thai Noodle Bar.

The other customer, an elderly square woman in a mustard-yellow coat sniffed disapprovingly. 'Don't know why they have to bring in all this foreign food. Nothing wrong with good old steak and kidney pie, if you ask me.'

The girl behind the counter grinned at Judy. 'Mavis doesn't like change, do you? My boyfriend went to Thailand and he says the food's really good. I'd try a noodle bar.'

'I'd give it a go.' Judy wanted to join in but not take sides, 'but I don't think I'll have time for a while.' The other two waited expectantly. 'We've just bought the guest house on the hill,' she explained, 'so I'm going to be pretty busy for a while.'

'Oh, White Oaks?' Mavis looked her up and down and Judy felt she was being judged as a piece of horseflesh. Were her fetlocks up to running up and down all those stairs? 'Those houses were all hotels when I was young. Now, they're all flats. Yours is the only one left.'

Judy brandished her postcard. 'Yes, I was wondering if I could put this in the window. My husband's had to go away unexpectedly and I need some staff.'

Mavis gave her a knowing look. 'Unexpectedly eh? Why?'

Lisa behind the counter shook her head. 'Mavis, don't be so nosy!'

'Oh, no, it's okay.' Judy felt herself blushing. 'He's in the Merchant Navy and he's had to go back to sea sooner than we thought so I need a chambermaid or two. Quickly,' she added.

Mavis drew herself up to her full five feet as she turned to Judy. 'You need me,' she told her.

'I do?'

'I've done cleaning all my life. You won't find anyone better than me. I'm reliable and I know what I'm doing.' Judy wished she didn't feel intimidated. Mavis would undoubtedly do the job brilliantly, but she might take over. 'What I'll do is come back up with you now and see what has to be done, then we can tackle it together.'

Hold on! Hold on! She hesitated, playing for time. She thought about Jan coming down and decided she could do with a bit of back-up. 'That won't work. I'm not going straight home, I've a few other things to do first.' Judy realised she wouldn't get off that lightly. 'Why don't you come and have a cup of tea this afternoon and then we can talk about it?'

'About three?'

Judy nodded weakly. 'Make it three thirty.' Jan must be down by then.

'I'll be there.' Mavis turned on her heel, clearly a woman on a mission. 'Bye Lisa!' She left and Judy realised she'd been holding her breath.

She and Lisa looked at each other. 'She's fierce!' exclaimed Judy.

'She is,' agreed Lisa, 'but her heart's in the right place.'

'Well,' Judy felt she needed to reserve judgement on that one. 'I'll need someone else as well, so can I still put the card up?'

They agreed that the card should stay up for a week and Judy trudged back up the hill.

She'd only been in the house ten minutes when the phone rang.

'Hello, I hear you're looking for a chambermaid.'

'Gosh! That was quick.'

'I'm Lisa's sister.' The girl paused. 'Lisa, you know, from the newsagent.'

'Oh, right.' Judy marvelled at how well the small-town grapevine worked. 'Well, what's your name?'

'Kelly. I'm sixteen so I can only work evenings and weekends but I'll be really quick and I promise I'll always turn up.'

'Why aren't you at school now?'

'I am. I've just nipped out of Drama to call you. Lisa texted me after you'd been in the shop.'

'Right. Well, come and see me after school

and we'll talk about it.'

'Thank you. Thank you ever so much. I promise you won't regret giving me a chance. See you then, Byeee!'

If the effectiveness of staff could be judged by their keenness, then Judy reckoned her two recruits were going to be the best chambermaids ever.

Reaching for the kettle, she decided she deserved a cup of coffee to fortify herself. Then, she'd better have a walk round the rooms and make sure that they were up to what she was sure would be Mavis's exacting standards. She realised she'd already become fond of the house. She wanted Mavis to like it too, and Jan.

Her tour of inspection was not reassuring. They couldn't use the three top rooms as the roofer wouldn't say when he could start work and the roof leaked into them. The next floor down was better. Five rooms in reasonable condition, though the bathrooms needed a serious scrub and the two family rooms on each half-landing in between were okay, though there were some dubious stains on the carpet and unidentified liquids had been spilt over the wallpaper. However, there was not a single room that she could show people with any sense of pride.

At three thirty the doorbell rang. Hoping it was Jan, Judy went to answer it with a barking Bosun at her feet. This was another problem she'd have to address. It would drive both her and her guests mad if the dog barked every time the bell rang.

She could see Mavis' yellow coat through the stained glass of the Victorian front door so she opened the door with some trepidation. Mavis stood there with Jan behind her, making faces guaranteed to make Judy laugh. She tried to contain the giggle into a smile and, realising that she probably looked totally deranged, invited them both in while trying to introduce them to each other.

'Hello, Mavis, good of you to come. This is Jan, my friend. Jan, this is Mavis, she's going to come and clean for me, I hope. Get the place into some sort of order.'

'Great! If you point me in the direction of the kitchen, I'll put the kettle on. Or,' Jan glanced at Judy, 'shall we go straight to wine?'

'Tea, I think at this stage.' Judy winked at Jan, indicating Mavis who, she was quite sure, would disapprove strongly of anyone drinking wine in the middle of the afternoon. 'Jan, you can have the guided tour later, so shall I show you round, Mavis?'

'Best if you just give me the master keys and I'll have a look round myself. I know the building. Worked here twenty-five years ago for Eric and Margaret. Nice couple they were.'

Judy was already feeling inferior and Mavis wasn't helping. 'The rooms aren't locked. Just help yourself. How do you take your tea?'

'White, two sugars. Strong.' And Mavis hung her yellow coat over the banisters and headed off upstairs while Judy and Jan went through the breakfast room to the kitchen.

'Where did you get her?' Jan spluttered as they giggled like naughty schoolgirls who'd been caught by teacher. 'She's scary.'

'I know, but she might be just what I need. I'm just going to have to be brave enough to tell her what to do.' Jan poured the tea into mugs as the bell went again, followed by a volley of barking from the sitting room.

'That'll be Kelly. This could be tricky. Shut up, Bosun!'

Kelly was already in the hall when Judy went out there. 'The door was on the latch. Hi, I'm Kelly. This is really good of you to give me a job.'

‘Well, let’s see how we get on.’ Judy was sure she hadn’t promised Kelly work, but maybe she had implied that. What would Mavis say? ‘Come into the kitchen and have a cup of tea.’

‘I don’t drink tea, but I’ll have a glass of water if you don’t mind.’ Kelly looked up the stairs. ‘This is a really big place, isn’t it?’

‘Twelve rooms, and they all need some work.’

‘I’ll bet they’re nicer than some places in Sandhaven. My sister, not Lisa the other one, she worked at a place where there were mice and no one did anything about it.’

Judy laughed, ‘I don’t think I’ve got mice. I’ve got a dog that wouldn’t stand for that.’

‘Oh, I love dogs. Can I meet it?’

‘Later. First of all, come and meet my friend Jan who’s staying with me at the moment and Mavis, who you might be working with.’

‘Oh, I know Mavis. Everybody in Sandhaven knows Mavis. She’s okay.’ Judy breathed a sigh of relief. That was one hurdle crossed.

Mavis was already back in the kitchen when Judy took Kelly in.

‘Hello, Kelly. Didn’t realise you knew Judith.’

'Judy.' No one called her Judith except her mother and if Mavis started behaving like her mother then she really couldn't work here.

'I'm going to be a chambermaid here.' Kelly announced and Judy cringed.

'Good,' said Mavis, 'you can do the running around while I apply the elbow grease. We'll make a good team.' She ran an expert finger along the underside of the worktop. 'There's a lot to do.'

Jan and Judy exchanged glances, and Judy shrugged her shoulders. That appeared to be one problem solved.

'When are your first guests due?' Mavis was very business-like.

'It's Wednesday today. I've got a party of ten divers coming in next Thursday and then some walkers immediately afterwards for the weekend.'

'Plenty of time to get you straight then.' Judy was extraordinarily comforted to realise that she wasn't on her own any more.

They all drank tea round the kitchen table while Kelly and Mavis worked out how they'd share the load. Kelly would work weekends and Mavis weekdays, once they'd got the place shipshape, and then they'd both give Judy a hand with breakfast when needed.

'Sounds like I've got my team.' Judy wondered what Gordon's reaction would be to this fait accompli but, given the circumstances, he could hardly comment.

'Of course, there will be a bit less work once my husband's home.' She thought she ought to mention him, just so that they remembered he existed. After all, this was half his business.

'I think your husband will have enough to do in this place without getting under our feet.'

Mavis had a point.

They agreed payment terms and Judy just hoped she'd get enough guests in to cover the wages. She could see a huge black hole looming in their finances once the roofer put his bill in and the amount of work to do was truly daunting.

'Now, Kelly and I will just go upstairs and have a look through the linen cupboard so we can give you a list of what we need. We'll make up a couple of rooms too, so you can see what they'll look like when they're done.'

'Great,' Judy was glad to let someone else take some responsibility. 'If you're making up rooms, can you do number three? Jan's gong to be in there for the next couple of nights.'

'Will do. But that's a cold room. She'd be better in Four.'

Judy capitulated meekly.

Mavis and Kelly went off upstairs and Judy gave Jan a tour of inspection, starting off with downstairs and working their way round the building.

When they came back to the kitchen Jan was uncharacteristically quiet.

'What do you think?' Judy broke the silence.

Jan spoke slowly. 'I think it's a fabulous house, and Sandhaven looks like a wonderful place, but I'd be seriously scared of the amount you've got to do.'

'That's what I think too. Gordon doesn't seem to be worried by it. He just says we can work our way round the building and, in the meantime, we can stay open and make some money, but I don't think it's going to be as easy as that.'

'Particularly if he's not here,' Jan pointed out. She stretched. 'Forget the fish and chips. We'll go out for supper tonight – on me. So, we can get in a couple of hours work, have a glass or two of this plonk I brought and then we'll go and savour the delights of Sandhaven.'

'Um, Gordon might phone tonight. He

normally calls when he gets to the ship.'

'Well, he'll have to leave a message, won't he? Once you're open you won't be able to get out much. Let's make the most of it before you start having guests. Kitchen first?'

'Yes, but I'd better just go and see what those two are up to.'

Judy went upstairs to the riot of colour that was room four where Mavis was instructing Kelly on exactly how to clean a bathroom. 'Right in the corners, there. That'll all come off if you scrub.'

The bed was made up, the furniture polished and although the room still looked shabby, it was clearly clean and cared for. Perhaps they could get away with this for a while.

'Hey, that looks better.'

'We'll come and do the rest of them over the next few days before you open,' Mavis announced. 'You won't know the place when we've finished.'

Kelly peered out from the bathroom. 'Is this okay, Mavis?' she asked, and Mavis went off to check.

'Oh,' she paused and glanced at Judy over her shoulder. 'I've made a list of the linen I reckon you need. There's a place in Bournemouth that specialises in contract stuff for hotels. I'll get you the name of it.'

'Fine,' Judy agreed submissively, 'Jan and I can go tomorrow. Thanks, Mavis.' But Mavis was already in the bathroom showing Kelly exactly what was wrong with the way she'd cleaned the basin.

Judy reflected that it was quite amazing what you could get done in a few hours if you were able to chat and laugh while you did it. She and Jan had scrubbed the kitchen walls and disinfected the worktops. The cupboards and drawers had all been emptied, half the contents thrown out and then, once everything was clean, re-packed so that Judy could find things. The kitchen now looked ready for action. It was still outdated and nothing could improve the yellow tiles on the walls, but at least she knew it was clean. They'd set the world to rights and discussed the children. When Jan pointed out that Lucy was sensible and in the end she wouldn't actually get engaged to Jason if it wasn't the right thing to do, Judy believed her. Judy told Jan that her parents wanted to come and visit.

'Your parents mustn't see the place like this.' Jan had met Judy's parents, Geoffrey and Rose, many times over the years and had always marvelled that they could have produced Judy. They were, she reckoned, the most snobby and elitist people she'd ever come across. 'They live on another planet. They simply wouldn't have a clue what you were doing here.' There was a pause as they both tried to imagine Rose in this kitchen. Impossible.

'We can cook now.' Judy commented. 'We could stay in tonight.'

'Pub!' said Jan in a tone that brooked no argument. 'Do any of the showers work?'

'Yes. Room Four's is okay, I think. In fact, that's one of the better bathrooms. Let me know whether it's really okay. I'll take you up.'

Jan grabbed her holdall from their private sitting room floor where Bosun was using it as a pillow and headed upstairs. Judy led her into a large, well-proportioned room with a high ceiling and big windows that gave a sideways view of the sea. The walls were covered in a busy pattern of big pink roses, set off by a bedspread covered in poppies. The effect was rather like an overgrown herbaceous border where everything had run riot. Jan put her holdall on the bed and the mattress sank visibly. 'Half an hour!' She instructed. 'I'll be down for a quick glass of wine and then we'll go out at seven.'

'Yessir!' Judy saluted as she ran down the stairs, collecting Bosun from the hall on the way. 'I've told you before. You stay out the back! Now, let's get you fed and then we're off to the pub. It's said to be dog-friendly so you can come too.'

It was eleven before Judy and Jan let themselves back into White Oaks. The pub had proved very friendly and was hosting a quiz, which they'd foolishly joined in. They hadn't done very well, but they'd laughed a lot and one drink had led to another. Bosun had made friends with Bailey, the pub Labrador, and the landlady, Sharon, had offered Judy any help she needed. They were exhausted but cheerful when they came in and Jan decided to make coffee before bed.

As they settled down with their mugs the phone rang. They'd been discussing Mavis and wondering about her love life and Judy was still laughing as she answered, 'White Oaks Guest House.' There was a slight delay on the line and she immediately realised that it must be a satellite phone. 'Gordon?'

'Jude? Just thought I'd let you know I'd arrived. You sound cheerful.'

'Been down The Anchor with Jan.'

'Jan's down?'

'Yes, she came down to help for a couple of days.'

'What's the pub like?'

'Great. We had such a laugh! It was quiz night. We weren't very good. We needed you!' Gordon was one of those people who seemed to absorb general knowledge by osmosis. He knew the most extraordinary things and was always an asset on quizzes and crosswords. 'Oh, and I've got some staff.'

'Blimey, I only left this morning.'

'Well, it kind of happened by accident. Mavis was in the shop when I went in to put the advert in the window and Kelly is Lisa's sister.'

'You've lost me completely.'

'Sorry, but it's honestly not worth explaining. When the computer's set up I'll email it all to you.'

'I'm not going to have a clue what's going on when I get back, am I?'

'Don't worry. There'll be plenty for you to do!' She kept her tone light but there was an edge to it that she just couldn't hide.

There was an awkward pause.

'Right then, well, I'll call you in a few days before we sail.'

'Okay. Love you,' the sign-off was automatic.

‘You too,’ and the line went dead with a firm click.

Jan had tactfully buried her head in a magazine to avoid appearing to eavesdrop. She looked up. ‘How is he?’

Tears sprung to Judy’s eyes. ‘A long way away.’

Jan reached for the bottle, still half full from earlier, and filled their glasses while Bosun climbed onto Judy’s lap.

The talk turned to their plans for the next day; more cleaning and a pushy phone call to the roofer to tie him down to a date, followed by a trip to Bournemouth to buy some linen.

They had just decided that opening another bottle of wine would be downright irresponsible and bed was a better and more sensible option when there was an almighty crash which made both of them leap from their chairs and stare at each other in terror. Bosun rushed behind a pile of boxes and peered out, barking furiously.

‘What the…? What was that?’ Jan was the first to speak.

‘I don’t know. But it sounded expensive!’

The noise seemed to have come from the so-called conservatory behind their sitting room. Judy opened the door with trepidation. A window frame lay on the floor surrounded by broken glass and yet more of Gordon and Judy's boxes, which had yet to make it into the house. There was a gaping hole in the perspex roof.

'A window must have fallen out upstairs.' Jan was mystified. 'How the devil did that happen?'

'Mavis said she'd left the window in room seven open to try and get rid of the musty smell. The wind must have caught it. What on earth am I going to do about this?'

'Pray it doesn't rain tonight and put a tarpaulin over it tomorrow?'

'Fine idea. But I don't have a tarpaulin.'

As they stood there in the dark, Bosun suddenly started growling.

'Everything all right?' A man's voice came out of the gloom. 'I'm Peter from next door. Do you need a hand?'

'Well, I've got a hole in the conservatory roof. The conservatory wasn't up to much in the first place, but now it's completely useless, plus I've got a room upstairs with no window in it. Tell me it's not going to rain tonight!'

'I'll come over with my son and get a waterproof over the roof and a board over the window so you're weatherproof and then you can decide what to do next in the morning. I've been meaning to come over and say hello anyway.'

'I'd be so grateful if you would. Are you sure you don't mind?'

'Not at all. You ladies on your own there?'

Embarrassed that she had to explain again, Judy told him about Gordon being called back to sea. 'Well, I'm on my own in the garden flat next door. My son's just staying, passing through. Anything you need, just ask. Now don't you freeze, I'll just get Harry and we'll get this covered up in no time. You go on inside.'

'Would you like some coffee or a glass of wine?'

'No, thanks. You get inside. I'll come round in the morning and introduce myself properly but for now we'll just get you weatherproof.'

Judy and Jan obeyed orders and headed back inside. 'Wow, a real Sir Galahad,' Jan commented. 'That was lucky.'

'Mmm.'

'He seems nice.'

'He does. I just wish it was Gordon sorting it out.'

Jan yawned.

'You go off to bed, Jan. I'll just wait for

Peter and his son to finish.'

'Are you sure? I'm bushed. Not sure if it's using my brain in the quiz or the wine!'

'Probably has more to do with scrubbing my kitchen.'

There were thuds and mutterings from outside that signified activity. Judy roused herself and headed back out. It had just started to rain and she felt even guiltier. A big blue tarpaulin was stretched over the conservatory roof and Peter and his son were pulling on ropes either side to secure it.

'You two okay out there? Sure you wouldn't like something?'

'We're fine, my dear. Just got to get the ladder to get a board over the window and we'll be finished. Stay in the warm and I'll give you a knock when we're done.'

She sank into a chair and reflected that for a day that had started so badly, quite a lot had been achieved. Jan was here, that was the best bit. She had staff, friends down the hill at the pub and a nice neighbour. She sipped the dregs of her coffee and hoped that Peter and his son would finish soon. She could do with snuggling down under the duvet and forgetting everything until tomorrow.

She was just about to open the conservatory door to check on progress when there was a crash, a thud and a cry.

'Dad? Dad! You all right?'

'What's happened?' She was outside in the rain in an instant.

There was a dark form lying very still on the path outside the door.

'Quick!' A voice came from the garden. 'It's Dad. He's fallen off the ladder and hit his head. Call an ambulance.'

She rushed inside and picked up the phone, trembling as she punched in three nines.

'White Oaks Guest House, come quick. There's been an accident!'

Four

The First Arrivals

'Where can I hang my wetsuit?'

'There's ten of us. Where do you recommend for dinner?'

'I've got a problem with my weight belt. Can I borrow a screwdriver?'

'Any chance of an early breakfast? The boat goes out at nine.'

Judy, standing behind reception feeling vulnerable and battered, raised a hand and smiled. 'Hey, one at a time! There's a laundry down the side of the building. I'll get you the key and your wetsuits can go in there. The Anchor at the bottom of the hill does a nice meal and I'm sure Sharon will look after you.' She was pleased with that, it made her sound like a local and she could certainly recommend the food. Judy and Jan had eaten there a couple of times during Jan's brief stay to help her get ready for these, her first guests. 'Now, what else was it?'

'Screwdriver?' a large man reminded her

somewhat sullenly.

'Right, hang on for that. It'll take me a minute to track one down.'

'Early breakfast?' a little terrier of a chap who was clearly in charge leaned on the counter. 'You see, love, we need to be down on the pier at eight thirty.' Judy resisted the urge to tell him not to call her love and that she'd told him when breakfast was served when he'd phoned to confirm the booking. 'I'll let you know about the early breakfast, as soon as I've checked with the staff that they can come in. Now, let me just get your keys.'

She escaped through the door behind Reception into her own sitting room.

Things were improving in there. The boxes were unpacked and although she still couldn't find anything it was beginning to feel like home.

She'd already allocated the divers their rooms, three in each of the big family rooms and the other four split between the two best twin rooms on the first floor. This was the bit she was dreading. Although Mavis and Kelly had scrubbed everything they could and she'd bought new linen so that the beds felt crisp and fresh, she still knew that the rooms were downright scruffy.

She took a deep breath and went out to face the fray again. The lads were joking and bantering and seemed very big and noisy. She wished Gordon was here to help her handle this, but he was bobbing about in the Atlantic somewhere, delivering grain.

'Is the bar going to be open tonight, love?'

'I'm sorry, but we only moved in a couple of weeks ago and I just haven't had time to set it up.'

A quietly spoken man on the edge of the group chimed in. 'Don't worry. We'll go to the pub. That'll do us fine.'

She shot him a grateful glance. 'Thanks. Now, let me show you to your rooms and then I'll check on breakfast and find you a screwdriver. Just come down to Reception in ten minutes or so.'

None of them commented as she showed them into their rooms. She'd tried to make them attractive with flowers and new towels. She just hoped all the hot water worked. A plumber was supposed to be coming to check the whole system but, like everyone else in Sandhaven, he didn't seem to be in any rush to start work.

When she and Gordon had discussed the move, they'd hoped to enjoy a slower pace of life but she hadn't bargained for quite how frustrating it would be. If the weather was good, it seemed that tradesmen would rather go fishing than work or, if it was wet, a lot of them seemed to spend their days in the pub.

She ran back downstairs and wondered where there might be a screwdriver.

The back door into the conservatory attached to her sitting room opened and Peter from next door popped his bandaged head round the door. She sometimes wondered if he was either psychic or hung around outside waiting for her to need something.

'Hello! I've made a shepherd's pie and it's come up as more than I thought. I can't finish it. Just wondered if you'd like some.' He was brandishing a pie dish.

'Thanks, Peter. That'd be lovely. Sorry I can't stop but I've got my first group of guests checking in and they're demanding to say the least.' Since he'd fallen off her roof ten days ago, she'd seen a lot of Peter. It had been wonderful that he'd gone up the ladder to put a tarpaulin on her leaking conservatory and she'd been very grateful, but gratitude only went so far. She knew he was lonely but the habit he'd developed of popping in and out all the time had to stop.

'They want a screwdriver.'

He came into the sitting room and immediately found a few tools secreted behind a curtain. 'I put these on the window sill. Thought it wasn't worth putting them away as we were bound to need them.'

Alarm bells rang in Judy's head. Although it was very useful to have him around to do some of the things that Gordon, had he been home, would have tackled it was becoming obvious that he was dong his best to make himself indispensable.

Before she'd headed for home, Jan had warned her about Peter. 'Don't let him get his feet under the table. A lonely widower is all you need.'

'He means well and I can't help but feel bad about him.' Judy had countered mildly, but Jan was having none of it.

'Mark my words. He thinks he can worm his way in and you don't need that.'

'I'm a married woman. He's only trying to be neighbourly.'

'Hmmm.' Jan had snorted in a way, which made her views quite clear, and over the last few days Judy had realised that she'd have to be careful. She didn't want to upset him, but Gordon would be home in June and he wouldn't be impressed to find Peter popping in and out with proprietorial ease.

She thanked him and took the pie which would, she conceded, be useful. She'd been so busy getting ready for her first guests that she hadn't even thought about her own supper. Pausing only to phone Mavis and Kelly who were both coming in to help with her very first proper breakfast, she headed back to Reception.

The miserable man was waiting at reception and she handed over the screwdriver. He took it away without a word. The group leader appeared from the lounge.

'No problem with the early breakfast,' she announced.

He smiled. 'Great. Thank you.'

'What are you diving for?'

'There's a wreck out just beyond the bay. It's a cargo ship that went down just at the end of the First World War. Some of us have done it before, but it's a good training dive. Just hope the visibility's good when we get down there. It can be a bit spooky when the water's murky.'

'I can't imagine anything worse than being underwater in a confined space where you can't see properly.'

'It's exhilarating. Takes you out of yourself.' He turned for the stairs.

Judy shivered at the thought as she went

through to the kitchen to heat up the shepherd's pie.

After a while she heard the divers go out to dinner and she breathed a sigh of relief. Resisting the urge to sit down with a glass of wine, the dog on her knee and watch television, she turned her attention to the kitchen. If these divers wanted an early breakfast she needed to be absolutely ready. Fortunately there were only ten of them, no worse than a big meal at home when the children and their friends were all around. She made sure there was enough juice in the fridge, took the bread out of the freezer and checked that she had all the other ingredients for a proper English breakfast. Bacon and sausages, both from the local butcher, tomatoes and mushrooms, yoghurts, and an appetising bowl of fruit on the side in the dining room. She'd done the best she could.

There were a few rooms still to let and Judy half-hoped that no one would ring the bell for them. Ten was okay as a baptism; twenty might start to be a bit of a struggle. However, she knew she couldn't afford to turn away business.

Once she'd made all the preparations she could, she settled down to eat Peter's pie which, she had to admit, was delicious. She'd have to invite him in for supper to thank him for everything he'd done, but then he'd probably get the wrong idea. Oh, dear.

It occurred to her that it would actually be good, eventually, to get the bar open as it would give her a chance to meet her guests properly. Otherwise they were just going to check in, eat breakfast and go away. She'd pictured herself chatting to people and helping to make their break go well, but at this rate she'd just spend her time running around after them.

The doorbell startled her and, to a volley of barking and a cry of 'Shut up, Bosun', she answered the door to an elderly man in a mac and a battered Tilly hat.

'I'm looking for a single room for a couple of nights.'

She told him how much it would be, he filled in a registration form and she took him up to the first floor.

As she went downstairs she wondered what he would do all evening, whether he would stay in or go out. It seemed very odd that there were people coming and going, yet she had no idea who was in her own house. She supposed she would get used to it.

Another couple of rooms were let over the course of the evening and Judy developed a litany of what people needed to know: 'breakfast is between 8.30 and 9.30, don't smoke in your rooms, take your keys out with you…' She began to feel quite professional and confident.

At ten thirty, she went out the front, turned out most of the lights and carefully locked the door to her own accommodation. Reminding Bosun that he mustn't bark if he heard people come in late and wishing that Gordon was there to share their first proper night's trading, she went to bed, somewhat apprehensive about breakfast.

At ten o'clock the next morning, Judy insisted that Mavis and Kelly sit down and have a coffee to celebrate a successful start. Breakfast had been fine, a little slower than she would have liked but she'd worked out how to speed things up.

Mavis had taken the orders and made sure that the guests were happy out the front and Kelly, who fortunately had double games, which she was able to miss, on a Thursday morning, had run around making tea and toast, delivering meals, clearing tables and generally looking busy. Her enthusiasm and cheerfulness were infectious and as Judy had peeked through the window in the dining room swing door to see how it was all going, she'd even seen the man who, she remembered, still had her screwdriver, laugh and smile as his breakfast was delivered.

The single man had shed his mac and hat and now sported a jumper that had clearly seen better days. He sat alone at a table behind the door and worked his way through bacon, egg and tomato. Kelly said he looked dodgy, but then she also said that Screwdriver-man, who was apparently called Bob, was a bit of a babe under that tough exterior. Judy reckoned her taste was more than a little suspect.

She sent Mavis and Kelly upstairs to start on the rooms and surveyed the breakfast room. They had cleared the tables and the two aged dishwashers which, thankfully, worked, had been loaded. She couldn't relay the tables as there wasn't enough crockery to do the dining room twice. That was something else they needed to buy but it would have to wait.

A moment later Mavis appeared in the kitchen. 'There's a woman in the hall says she wants a room. I wouldn't touch her with a barge pole myself. Snooty type. They're all the same; she's got her nose so far in the air I'm surprised she doesn't walk into things. She'll moan about everything. You don't need ones like her.'

'I'll come out.' Judy followed Mavis into the hall.

'Darling!' Judy's mother erupted into the hall in a cloud of Chanel No.5. 'We've been down in Devon and we're on our way to visit Reg and Margaret in Henley. I thought it would be fun to pretend to be a guest!'

'Mum, Dad! How nice.' This was all she needed. Her mother would expect everything to stop for her and Judy just hadn't got time. She'd planned to invite her parents in a month or two when things had settled down and she knew what she was doing.

The phone rang and Judy took it from her pocket. 'Shan't be a minute!'

'Judy, it's Sharon from the pub.'

'Hi, Sharon.'

'First of all, I wanted to thank you for sending the group of chaps down to eat last night. They were good fun! If I get any enquiries for accommodation I'll make sure they come your way. May as well do each other a good turn where we can.'

'Great! Thanks.' Judy felt a small satisfying glow at becoming part of the Sandhaven tourism mafia. She began to feel as though she belonged, but that all disappeared with Sharon's next question.

'You don't have an elderly man in a grey mac and a hat staying do you?'

'Er, yes actually. Why?'

'Oh, we have a ring-round system from the local police. They phone one person and then we all call each other. Beth from The Riviera has just called and apparently someone left a guest house in Corfe Castle without paying. I gather he caused a bit of damage too. They implied he has problems.'

'What! Oh, no, what do I do now?'

'I suggest you call the local station and ask them. How did your first breakfast go by the way?'

'Fine, actually. Not bad at all,' but Judy was distracted and conscious of her mother and Mavis listening in. 'I'd better go.'

'Mmm. Let me know what happens. Bye.'

'I don't suppose there's a chance of some coffee?' Her mother had never been able to work out when it was better to just melt into the background if people were busy.

'Um, yes, in a minute.'

Mavis stepped in. 'I'll do it. You go on up young Kelly, you can do the running around.' Kelly obediently headed for the stairs, bucket in hand.

'Thanks, Mavis. Mum, why don't you come and sit in the lounge. I'll come and have coffee with you in a minute. There are just a couple of things I have to sort out. Dad, the kitchen's that way, give Mavis a hand with the drinks!' Her dad would like Mavis, she knew, and he always welcomed an opportunity to talk to someone other than her mother.

'That's fine, dear. You're a working girl. You do what you have to do. I'll go through and help what's-her-name with the coffee.'

An awful thought struck Judy. 'You're not planning on staying are you?'

'Oh, no, dear.' Rose looked around as only she could. 'Reg and Margaret are expecting us just after lunch. We're staying with them till the weekend.' For once, Judy was glad that the hall was so shabby.

Judy tried to install her mother in the guests' lounge, which was tatty but passable, but Rose laughed. 'I'm not a guest, dear, I'm family. Is this your flat through here?' She pointed to the door marked Private behind Reception. 'I'll go and see young Bosun.'

Judy gave up and ran upstairs to start sleuthing. 'Is the man in Room One still in?'

'No, he went out. He could have tidied his

room a bit! Right mess he left us.' Kelly was indignant. 'Told you he was no good.'

Judy decided it would be best not to share her information. She didn't want to cause an unnecessary panic. She ran downstairs to call the police.

In her own accommodation she found her mother having coffee with Peter who'd obviously arrived for his morning drink.

'Judy was marvellous. Came and picked me up from hospital and everything. On the mend now, though.' Peter was clearly regaling Rose with the tale of the conservatory roof.

'How awful for you. You poor thing!'

'This place is a madhouse,' muttered Judy as she grabbed the cordless phone and went into the dining room, carefully shutting the door behind her so no one could hear.

She was glad she'd had the foresight to program the number for the police station into the phone. She got through to a very helpful sergeant who asked her to check the registration document for a name. She had a look and came up with about four different possibilities from the illegible hieroglyphics.

'We'll send someone straight up to see you.'

In her sitting room, Judy was delighted to find her parents apparently about to leave.

'You've only just arrived,' she protested half-heartedly.

'Oh, we're not off yet. I want a good look round the hotel but you're busy at the moment and I need a present for Reg's birthday. Peter here says there's a very good shop with unusual stuff down in the town.'

'"Curiosity" it's called. You're bound to find something there.'

'Back soon, then, darling. Come on, Geoffrey!' And she swept out.

Peter sat down again in what she'd come to think of as his armchair. 'Nice woman! You're very like her.' Judy was rendered speechless for a moment and was saved by the doorbell.

Two policemen stood at Reception and she brought them through to her sitting room. Peter rose.

'Peter,' she began.

'Hello, Richard,' he acknowledged the sergeant. 'Everything okay? I'll pop back later, Judy.'

Bosun was greeting the policemen as long lost friends, bouncing around them and leaving tiny white hairs on their uniform trousers.

'Bosun, down!' Judy scolded and the little

terrier scuttled back to his bed, watching with his head between his paws.

She offered them coffee, but the officers declined and perched on the edge of the sofa.

'First question,' she began. This was the one that had really been bugging her, particularly with Mavis and Kelly upstairs. 'Is he dangerous? If it's him, that is.'

'Not so far, though the place where he lives says he can become agitated if crossed.'

'I don't believe this. You know this is my very first day in business and I have the police round. Did you leave the car outside? I'll have half the neighbourhood wondering who's moved in.'

'We walked. You're okay.' The one called Richard smiled at her. 'Mind you, in this town everyone will know we're here in minutes. I've never worked out how the grapevine works but it's uncanny how quickly word gets round.'

His colleague agreed. 'And what they don't know, they'll make up,' he added.

'Small town life, eh? Well, that's what we wanted.'

'So, is the gentleman concerned in the building?'

'Not sure. I haven't said anything to the girls yet, didn't want to cause a panic if there was no need.'

'Very wise. Let's just check the registration form first, shall we? See if that throws any light on anything.'

They went through to Reception but none of them could decipher the name. 'Thomas? Thompson? That could even be a J. Johnson? And as for the address, it could be anything.'

'Not much point in the forms if you can't read them,' the policeman pointed out. 'You'll have to ask them to write more clearly.'

'I'll remember that for the future, but it doesn't help us now, does it.'

'We'd better go up and have a look at the room, then.'

'The girls said it was a bit of a mess.'

'Well, you should see what he did to the one in Corfe. A bit of a mess is an understatement.'

As they went through into the hotel hall, Mavis and Kelly came downstairs. Mavis greeted the sergeant as an old friend, 'Richard! What are you doing here?'

'Routine, Mavis.'

Kelly had gone bright red. 'It's not about the light on my bike, is it?'

The sergeant laughed. 'No, it's not. You're

Lisa's sister, aren't you?'

'That's me.'

'Word to the wise, young lady. Tell that sister of yours to steer clear of young Terry Philpot. She doesn't need to be around him and his mates.'

'I'll tell her, not that it'll make much difference.

'So, what are you here for?' Mavis, direct as ever, was determined not to be left out.

'The gentleman in Room One. Is he in?'

Kelly grinned triumphantly. 'Told you he was dodgy!'

'Kelly!' Judy warned, 'don't jump to conclusions. Is he there, though.'

'He came in a few minutes ago with some carrier bags.' Mavis was scathing.

Mavis and Kelly headed towards the kitchen. They'd obviously awarded themselves a coffee break.

There was the sound of a door opening upstairs and the elderly man from room one appeared on the stairs.

The police backed into the dining room doorway out of sight and Judy caught him as he reached the bottom of the stairs.

'I'm sorry,' she began, 'but I can't quite read your registration form. What's your name?'

'Thompson,' he replied, 'with a P in the middle.'

She realised no one had told her the name she was looking for, so she carried on, making her tone deliberately conversational. 'And what brings you to Sandhaven then?'

A police radio crackled into life in the dining room. 'Runaway apprehended.' Judy heard. 'Red Lion Public House. He threw his breakfast over the waitress and shouted abuse. Publican restrained him but backup required.'

The elderly man didn't seem to hear the radio, or presumed it was nothing to do with him. 'I'm glad I've seen you.' He looked embarrassed. 'I spilt some stuff in my room this morning. If you let me have a cloth, I'll clear it up.'

'No need.' Judy was so relieved that he wasn't the wanted man she could have hugged him. 'We'll see to that.'

Mr Thompson started towards the front door, but was almost knocked over as two policemen erupted from the dining room and rushed out of the front door, almost colliding with the divers coming in.

'You're back early.' Judy was fairly sure their rooms weren't ready yet.

'Got a gap between dives,' screwdriver-man explained. 'Just come up to shed some gear. We're back in the water this afternoon.'

One of the younger men came in behind him. 'It was amazing. I've never done a sea dive before. You really could imagine her when she was a working ship. All the different rooms and decks are still intact. She was carrying perfume.' Kelly crossed the hall with her coffee mug as he reached into his pocket and produced a tiny glass bottle. He handed it to her. 'Look!'

'Wow,' Kelly took it in amazement. 'How old is this?'

'Well, the ship went down in 1918.'

'That's amazing!' Carefully, she unscrewed the top. 'It still smells good!'

He blushed. 'You can have it if you like. I've got another one.'

'Hey, thanks.' She gave him a peck on the cheek and he went bright red.

Mavis appeared at the lounge door. 'Don't you dare put wet stuff in our rooms,' she said authoritatively. She looked at Judy. 'We have a rule, don't we? Wetsuits and other gear have to be stored in the laundry down the side of the building.'

'That's right.'

The divers trooped out again like naughty schoolboys, heading round the building to do as they were told.

Judy paused to catch her breath, but her mother appeared at the front door. 'Hello, dear, there's a rough crowd of men down your side passage and two policemen are outside running down the hill. What sort of a place is this?'

'You're back quickly, Mum.'

'Tacky little shop.' Rose dismissed it, 'but I did manage to find a rather nice vase that'll do the trick.'

Judy sighed.

'You've lost weight.' Rose looked at her critically, 'mind, that won't do you any harm.'

Judy wished Jan was here; she'd always had the knack of gently putting Rose in her place.

The divers, minus their kit, began to traipse back in again and Rose was pinned against the wall as they stampeded past her.

'Darling, they all look very – er – male? Whatever would Gordon say about all these hulks in your house?'

Screwdriver-man grinned, and Judy wondered if perhaps Kelly was right about him after all.

'Mum, they're just guests. Now, if you go in the lounge I'll be with you in a minute.'

The main-man of the dive group came

back down the stairs. 'Sorry to disturb you, love, but the lads wondered if you had any room later in the year? We'd like to book the whole place for the third weekend in September? It might not be the smartest place we stay, but it's definitely one of the friendliest.'

Delighted to escape, and thrilled that her guests were pleased, Judy went to check the diary, pausing as she noticed that the first entry had been made in the smart new Visitors' Book. 'Great room, lovely breakfast. Friendly people. John Thompson.'

Judy grinned.

The front door opened, and Peter burst into the hall, covered in oil; even his bandage had black fingermarks on it. 'Judy, can I borrow your shower room.' He had a flannel in his hand. 'Sharon's car broke down and she asked me to help. I got it going but I've got a hospital appointment and I can't go like this.'

'Um. Yes, of course. But you have your own shower?'

Judy knew she was blushing, although there was no reason. It was just the look on her mother's face.

'Plumber's in fixing a small leak. My water's turned off.'

Judy laughed. 'It's one of those days. Help yourself, you know where to go.' He went whistling through to her quarters but was back in a moment. 'Where's Bosun? He's not in here?'

'What? He must be!'

Rose looked troubled. 'I might have left the door open when I went to the shop.'

'Oh, Mum!'

Her father intervened. 'I'm sure he'll turn up, love. He's a sensible little chap.'

'No, he's not. He's got no road sense and once he gets his nose on a scent he'll go for miles. Oh, Mum, how could you?'

'Darling, I didn't mean to.'

'No, of course, you didn't. You never mean to. It just happens!' She called upstairs. 'Mavis, Kelly. The dog's gone. Can you hold the fort while we go out hunting?'

Mavis peered over the banisters. 'Kelly can come with you. I'll finish off here.'

Rose looked doubtfully at her watch. 'We'd better get off. We'll phone tonight to see what happens.'

'Whatever! Come on!' Judy was struggling into her jacket, tears in her eyes. Peter was all concern. 'Don't worry, Peter. You get off to the hospital.'

'No, I'll cancel. It's only a check-up!'

‘A kiss, darling?’ Rose presented a rouged cheek.

‘Mum, I’ve got to go. Ring me later! Come on, Kelly! We’ve got to find him, he’s Gordon’s dog!’ Leaving her parents, she ran out of the front door.

The road was deserted. Absolutely no sign of a small black and white terrier.

‘Bosun! Bosun! Oh, Bosun, where are you?’

Five

A Walk on the Wild Side

'Darling, I'd hoped I wasn't going to have to write this,' Judy sat at the keyboard wondering how to explain to Gordon that her mother, who was not his favourite person anyway, had accidentally left the door open and let his dog out. That was two days ago and there had been no sign of Bosun since. She'd just have to be blunt. 'Bosun has been missing for two days. My mother turned up unexpectedly and...' Even as she wrote, Judy knew that Gordon was going to be livid – and, in this instance, justifiably so. She couldn't find the words to cushion the blow and as she signed off with love and hit the send button, she sighed. The email was now winging its way to somewhere in the middle of the Atlantic and Judy would just have to wait for the eruption it was bound to generate.

The bar bell rang and as she went to answer it she reflected that she was pleased she'd got the bar up and running. The walking group who'd arrived earlier had arranged to meet for a drink before they went out. It wasn't yet very well stocked, but at least it offered her guests another facility and gave her the chance of some human contact. Also it took her mind off a cold Jack Russell terrier sheltering miserably somewhere. Why, oh why, didn't he just come home?

A few moments later, Judy wondered if her guests were going to stage a riot. They were gathered in the bar being briefed about their walk the next day by Stan, who was quite clearly in charge.

'So, it's twenty seven miles. Judy here,' she smiled on cue, 'is going to give us an early breakfast at half past seven and we'll all meet out the front at eight o'clock.'

A rather flabby man in a pullover that must have been knitted by his auntie put down his half of bitter. 'I'm sorry, Stan, but I'm not sure that I can walk twenty seven miles. I didn't realise it was going to be so strenuous.'

'I did tell everyone the length of the walks before we came away.' Stan was clearly not impressed by any slackers in the group, but the rebellion was gathering force. Two or three others were muttering about getting the bus back and it was clear that Stan had over-estimated the enthusiasm of his members.

'How hilly is the walk, Stan?' A younger, rather earnest looking chap in glasses was looking worried.

'Fairly.' Stan pulled out his map and spread it on the table, and an animated discussion about contour lines followed.

'I think we should just go for it.' A loud voice boomed out from the scrum and Judy picked out a youngish chap in a rugby shirt. 'We're all supposed to be fit. I'm up for it!' He looked very confident and a few of the doubters looked reassured.

Judy, behind the bar, clutched a half of lager for dutch courage. The plan had always been for Gordon to run the bar, but she realised that she was actually quite enjoying it.

'So how did you all get together,' she asked the nearest man.

'We all worked together at a pizza factory. They closed it down and we all went our separate ways, but we've kept in touch and we try to go away for a weekend once a year. It probably wouldn't happen without Stan, but he contacts everyone. It's usually a good laugh.'

'So, how far do you usually walk?'

'Something between twenty and thirty miles the first day. A whole lot less the second one!'

She smiled. 'Well, it's beautiful countryside round here. I'm sure you'll enjoy it and the forecast's good.'

The front door banged and Judy frowned. 'Excuse me.' She wasn't expecting any more guests and was quite happy with the fifteen she had. She went through her sitting room, noting painfully the lack of a small bouncing terrier to greet her, and through to Reception.

She gave a shriek of glee. 'Lucy! What a lovely surprise!' Judy lifted the flap on the reception desk and hurried to hug her daughter. 'Why didn't you say you were coming? Is Jason with you?'

'Don't mention that idiot!' Lucy's face made it quite clear that questions would not be welcome. 'I was sitting on my own in the flat and I thought I might as well come down. See what you've bought and how you're doing without Dad.' She paused, as the hubbub from the bar grew. 'Who's in there?'

'Guests. It's a hotel!'

'Men!' Lucy's eyes twinkled. 'Dad's hardly

back at sea and you've shipped a whole load of men in.'

'Hardly. They're a walking group. Come and have a drink!'

'Have you got a room I can have?'

Mentally, Judy went round the hotel rooms. 'There's a small double at the top of the house not in use. It's not the best room but it's all there is.'

'Whatever. When can I do a tour of inspection?'

'Not till tomorrow really, because the rooms are occupied. Come on and have a drink in the bar and we'll talk properly when this lot all go out to supper.'

The bar went quiet as Lucy walked in. She'd always turned heads and as she'd grown up she had a confidence and polish that Judy really envied.

'Hi, guys!' She swung her blonde hair and the chap in the rugby shirt immediately got to his feet.

'Drink?'

'It's all right,' Judy explained, 'Lucy's my daughter. Gin and tonic?'

Lucy nodded as she settled on a bar stool and in no time at all was on first name terms with them all. Even Stan appeared to have recovered from his fit of pique. Lucy's reaction when the length of the walk came up caused considerable mirth. ‘Twenty seven miles! How many days are you doing it in?’

Stan grinned. ‘Just the one.’

‘You’re mad. The whole lot of you. Stark staring crazy.’

Rugby Shirt, who turned out to be an accountant called Keith, did his macho bit again. ‘We’ll be fine, just you see!’

They downed their beers and headed upstairs to change before going out to eat and Lucy turned to her mother.

‘Hey, this is quite fun. Couldn’t imagine you behind a bar but it suits you.’

‘Thanks! Look Luce, I’ll show you to your room and then rustle up some pasta or something and we’ll catch up on all the news. There’s a lot to tell you.’

They went through into the private sitting room.

‘Where’s Bosun?’

‘That’s the first thing. He ran off two days ago. Mum let him out.’

‘Granny was down here? Wow, what did she make of all this?’ Lucy looked at the room which, Judy knew, left a lot to be desired. ‘Have you told Dad about Bosun? He’ll go berserk!’

'Tell me about it. I've emailed him, but I haven't heard from him yet.'

'Ouch. Be afraid, Mum, be very afraid.'

'I know. I wish he'd get in touch. He's not going to be happy.'

'Understatement of the year.'

'Well, it's not as though I did it on purpose. In fact, it's not as though I did it at all.'

'And you think the fact that it was Granny will help? Get real, Mum!'

Judy knew that Lucy was right on all counts, but she didn't need to have it pointed out to her. She wished Gordon would just reply and get it over with.

Lucy didn't comment as Judy showed her to her room.

'We've got a lot of work to do,' she knew she was babbling, 'but at least they're clean and so far the guests have been quite happy.'

'Well,' Lucy threw her smart leather hold-all onto the bed, 'that's all right then, isn't it? I'm just going to have a quick shower – wash that man right out of my hair – and then I'll be down. I'm starving actually.'

'I'll rustle up some pasta and you can tell me about Jason. If you want to, that is.'

'Basically, Mum, he's arrogant and self-ish.'

Judy felt it wiser not to agree at this stage. 'I'll see you downstairs,' and she escaped to the kitchen.

Half an hour later, Judy was still trying to find time to put the pasta into the pan. She'd boiled the water and opened a jar of sauce to go with it but the bell kept ringing every time she tried to finish the job.

'Home cooking at its best,' Lucy wandered into the kitchen, colliding with Judy as she ran to answer yet another query. She'd so far provided a pencil, spare laces for a pair of walking boots (pure luck that one) and directions to the nearest confectioner for someone who claimed, quite rightly Judy thought, that he couldn't possibly walk twenty seven miles without several bars of chocolate.

'Just pop the pasta in, and put the bowls in the oven – oh, and grate the cheese and then we're there.'

Judy found Stan waiting at Reception. 'Have you got a needle and thread? The button's fallen off my favourite shirt. It's the one I wear when I lead a walk.' Judy wondered what happened when he went away walking for a week. Same shirt every day? It didn't bear thinking about but she found her sewing kit and he went away happy.

Judy breathed a sigh of relief as she heard the walkers head out to dinner, and she dished up the pasta into the bowls, sprinkled the cheese and headed for the sofa in her private quarters where they could eat off their laps.

'Any wine, Mum? A nice full-bodied red would wash this down a treat.'

'Mmm,' Judy swallowed her mouthful quickly. 'There's an open one in the bar.' She put her bowl on the table, realising with a pang that she could leave it there without the fear of a small nosy Jack Russell stealing it in her absence.

'So, what happened with Jason?'

'Oh, I'm not sure I really want to talk about it.' Lucy paused and Judy waited. 'Basically it was all over something pretty stupid. He wanted me to go to a company thing of his on a night I'd arranged to go out with the girls. If it was only once I wouldn't mind, but…'

The back door opened and Peter from next door walked straight in.

Judy thought for the umpteenth time that she really must put a stop to this and make him come round the front and ring at Reception like everyone else.

'Hello,' he came in right hand outstretched

to Lucy who was trying to balance a bowl on her lap and free a hand to shake at the same time. 'You must be Lucy. I've heard a lot about you.'

'All good I hope.'

'Of course. I'm Peter Lorimer from next door. Your mother and I have become firm friends in a short time.' He turned to Judy. 'Now, I mustn't disturb your supper but I just wanted you to know that I've been out to the dog rescue and the terrier they've had brought in definitely isn't Bosun.'

'Damn.' Judy's eyes filled with tears.

Peter gave a rather hearty laugh. 'He'll turn up, you'll see.'

'Well, I wish he'd get on with it before Gordon contacts me.'

Peter perched on the arm of a chair, clearly settling in for a chat.

'Peter,' Judy had learnt that she just had to be blunt. 'I haven't seen Lucy for a while and we've got a lot to talk about.'

He leapt to his feet. 'Sorry. Of course, of course.' He turned to Lucy, 'your mother's been very kind,' he rubbed the side of his head, now mercifully unbandaged following his fall from her roof, 'but I mustn't outstay my welcome.'

Judy and Lucy said nothing and after a

pause, he let himself out.

'So, you were saying. Did you go to Jason's company do?'

'No, I went out with the girls and he sulked, but it's not the first time...'

The phone rang and Judy rose to take a booking from someone attending a wedding in the town, one room for now with the possibility of more. She sat down again.

'Go on.'

'Well, I'd already agreed to see the girls from where I used to work. It had taken a bit of organising and he sprung this on me at the last minute and expected me to drop everything. It just wasn't fair.'

The bell at Reception rang.

'I'm the last of the walkers. Had to work late. I'll just dump my stuff and go down and meet them. Do you know where they've gone for dinner?'

By the time Judy had shown him to the room he was sharing, organised a key for him and given directions to the pub where the others were, Lucy was in the kitchen loading the supper things into the dishwasher. 'I've thrown yours away, it was stone cold.'

Judy didn't like to tell her that she'd grown quite used to cold food. 'Right, let's finish that bottle of wine.'

They settled down at each end of the sofa again. 'So, back to Jason?'

'Oh, forget it Mum. I'm probably better off without him anyway.'

'Well, that's certainly what your father thinks.' Judy could have bitten her tongue. How could she have let that slip? They'd always been so careful not to comment on the children's romances.

Lucy went bright scarlet.

'Oh, Luce. I didn't mean that. It's just that...' the bell at Reception rang again and for once Judy was pleased to be rescued.

The sight of Jason at the Reception desk rendered her incapable of speech.

'Hello, Jude!' He was his usual cocky self. No one, but no one, except Gordon called her Jude.

'Jason!'

'I presume Lucy's here. We had a bit of a spat and she did her usual. Walked out. I thought she'd end up here.' He lifted the flap on the desk and walked through to Judy's private sitting room.

Judy stood back in amazement.

'Hi Lucy.'

'Jason! What the hell are you doing here.'

'Came to sort things out. Been a bit of an

idiot.' Judy shut the door on them and leant against it. Damn! Damn! Damn! Now they were going to get back together and Lucy would know her father's views on Jason. She'd probably guessed anyway but it was one thing to surmise and another to have it spelled out in black and white. Judy could have kicked herself.

She went and busied herself in the kitchen determined to keep out of the way and give Lucy a chance, hopefully, to tell Jason his fortune. Raised voices came from the sitting and Judy resisted the urge to listen.

She'd polished the cutlery, re-arranged the flowers in the dining room and emptied the dishwasher before Jason and Lucy appeared hand in hand. One look at the huge grin on her daughter's face told Judy all she needed to know.

'Sorted it out?' she asked casually.

'Yes! Silly misunderstanding!' Lucy looked adoringly at Jason and Judy resisted the urge to be sick or to remind her that she'd said she'd be better off alone. 'We're going to go for a walk on the beach. All right with you?'

'Of course. I presume you're both staying the night, then?'

'Yes, please.'

'Fine.' The happy couple went off and the

phone rang just as Judy was marvelling over the fickleness of the young.

'Has he turned up yet?' No hello, no nothing, just Gordon in ultra-efficient mode.

'Who?' Judy was still thinking about Lucy and Jason.

'My dog. The one your bloody mother allowed to escape in an area he doesn't know.'

Judy cringed. It was all as bad as she thought it would be. 'No, but we're all looking.'

'Who's all of us?'

'Well, the neighbours and Kelly and Mavis the chambermaids. They've all put feelers out. I'm sure he'll be back soon. I can't do any more about him anyway.'

'You could have looked after him better.'

'You could have been here to look after him yourself.' Oh, no! Twice in the same evening. Judy couldn't believe she'd said that.

'I don't exactly want to be here you know, when I could be home with you.'

'Lucy's here with Jason. He followed her down here. They'd broken up but it looks like they're back together.'

'Well that might have been one ray of sunshine in all this. What are your walking group like?'

'Nice. They've all been in the bar for a drink.'

'You've got the bar open? That was supposed to be my department.'

'Sorry, but people were asking for drinks. Think of the money.'

The line began to break up. 'This is going to go soon. Keep me posted on everything.'

'Will do! Gordon, I do love…' but the line was dead.

Judy went out the front to the deserted hotel. She sat on the stairs and looked around, daunted by the amount of work that had to be done and the fact that there was only her to do it, or at least arrange for it to be done.

She supposed she should wait up for Lucy and Jason, but they had a key and she felt physically exhausted and emotionally drained.

She locked up, hoping that all the walkers had remembered to take their keys with them and headed for bed, to dream of a Jack Russell terrier stuck down a rabbit hole barking and barking with no one to hear.

Breakfast the next morning was a busy affair with the hikers all wanting to stoke up before the walk ahead and when Lucy and Jason breezed into the kitchen half way through, Judy was brisk.

'Best thing is to sit in the dining room and pretend to be a proper guest,' she advised. 'There's not enough room for anyone else in here.'

'Good morning would be a start.'

Judy broke two eggs into a pan of boiling water. 'Sorry, love, just not at the moment.' The egg yolk broke. 'Grr! I hate poached eggs!'

Lucy disappeared through the swing door almost colliding with Kelly who was coming back with a tray full of used crockery.

'Wow, who's that?'

'That's my daughter, Lucy, and her boyfriend, Jason.' Kelly looked at Judy, clearly amazed, and Judy could guess her thoughts. How does this drab middle aged woman come to have such a stunning, sophisticated daughter?

'He's fit and she's gorgeous. Do you think she'd mind if I ask her where she got her jacket?'

'No, of course not.' Judy laughed, handing Kelly a couple of breakfasts to deliver. 'Just remember to take their order while you're at it.'

Jason and Lucy both ordered poached eggs on toast, Judy's pet hate. They took so long.

'Mind you,' she confessed to Mavis, who was folding yesterday's towels which had been in the tumble dryer over night, 'I suppose I might start eating muesli and poached eggs if I ended up looking like Lucy.'

'Too late for us, I think.' Mavis was less than five foot tall and roly-poly plump, but she had masses of energy and seemed fit as a fiddle.

The breakfast room emptied as the walkers evacuated to don their boots and head off for their ramble.

Finally only Lucy and Jason were left, lingering over their toast, and Judy took off her apron and, pouring herself a mug of coffee on the way, went to join them.

'So did you have a nice romantic walk along the beach then?'

'Mmm. Lovely. And Jason hadn't eaten so we had fish and chips sitting on the sea wall. Hope we didn't wake you when we came in, it was quite late.'

'No. Sorry I didn't wait up. This place doesn't allow late nights. I'm up at six thirty every morning.'

'Good God,' said Jason. 'That's the middle of the night.'

Judy laughed as the doorbell rang. She was just getting up to go and answer it, when Mavis passed. 'Stay put, I'll go.'

'Your father phoned last night. He's furious about Bosun.'

'Well, he would be. I did mention him to the walkers this morning. You never know, they might run into the little devil somewhere out on the hills.'

'Unlikely, but thanks anyway. I have a horrid feeling he's stuck somewhere. Gone after a rabbit and couldn't get out.'

'Oh, Mum, no. He'll starve.'

'Don't.'

Mavis clumped back into the dining room carrying a bouquet of flowers.

'Wow, Dad's gone over the top.'

'They can't be from him. He was livid and it's less than twelve hours since I spoke to him. He hasn't had time to organise them and somehow I don't think he feels like sending me flowers anyway.'

'Open the card, then.' Mavis tore the card from the cellophane and handed it to Judy.

'I just don't believe that woman! They're from my mother. "Sorry about the mishap. Hope the little chap's home safely. Thought these would brighten up the hotel. Love, Mum and Dad." She's incredible. Thinks a bunch of flowers can put anything right.'

Mavis sniffed. 'They're all the same, that sort. Think they can buy their way out of anything. I'll go and put these in water then we'd better get upstairs, young Kelly.'

Kelly clearly wanted to go on talking to Lucy but Mavis hustled her back to the kitchen and they headed off with laundry baskets full of yesterday's linen to put away.

'Mum, there's something I need to tell you.'

'Okay. Fire away.' The phone in Judy's pocket rang. 'Oh, bother, just a minute,' and she headed out the back to check the diary for availability at Easter. By the time she came back, Jason and Lucy had disappeared, presumably upstairs to their room.

She was soon immersed in the daily routine of loading dishwashers and washing machines, re-filling sugar bowls and jars of marmalade and honey and she jumped when Lucy came into the kitchen.

She had her coat on and was clearly ready to go. Jason was hovering behind her.

'Right, we're off!'

'Are you sure?'

'You've clearly got your hands full here. Frankly, Mum, I can't see how you're going to manage all this on your own and stay sane. It's obviously better if we get out of the way.'

Judy was about to protest when Peter arrived in the kitchen, coat on, and car keys dangling from one hand. 'Morning all. I'm going to go and walk on Studland Heath and see if there's any sign of the little blighter. Anyone want to come?'

Lucy threw Judy a pointed look. 'You don't have time for us at the moment. We'll give you a ring and book in as guests. Then we'll get priority.'

She leant forward and kissed Judy, as did Jason, then Lucy gave Peter a peck on the cheek which left him all flustered and they headed off.

'Successful visit?' Peter was clearly oblivious to the atmosphere.

'Not exactly. Look, give me half an hour to get everything sorted out here and I'll come with you. I could do with the exercise and Bosun's more likely to come to my call.'

After a fruitless day, Judy was despondent. She and Peter had walked the heath for hours, but the area was huge and Bosun could be anywhere. She was becoming resigned to the fact that he might not come back.

She made a cup of tea and sat down in the chair reviewing the last twenty-four hours. Gordon was furious with her. Lucy clearly felt neglected. Peter had told her what a wonderful day he'd had with her. In need of a friendly voice, she phoned Jan, but even she sounded strained.

'Hi, Jan, it's me.'

'Oh, Judy! Um, look, can I call you back?'

'Sure, bad moment?'

'Yes, kind of.'

'Okay. Nothing important anyway.'

An overwhelming tiredness came over her and she put her head back, eyes closed. The bell at Reception woke her and she came to with a start. She'd slipped her shoes off in her sleep and it took a second for her to gather herself sufficiently to go to the door.

At the desk was Stan, surrounded by his walking group, and in his arms was a very muddy Jack Russell Terrier. Judy burst into tears as she took the little dog in her arms.

'Oh, Bosun. Where've you been?' She kissed the top of his head and was rewarded with a lick as the little dog wriggled with excitement.

She looked up at the walkers, embarrassed by her tears.

'I guess it's him then?' Stan was grinning.

Judy nodded. 'Where did you find him?'

'One of the rangers had him. He was just about to bring him back to you. I think he said you'd emailed a photograph? We said we were staying here and offered to bring him home. He only had to walk the last five miles. Apparently the ranger heard him whimpering and dug him out of a hole first thing this morning when they were out bird watching at dawn.'

'Oh, thank you.' Relief flooded through her as the little dog settled in her arms with a deep contented sigh.

'You'll be covered in mud.'

'I don't care. I'm so pleased to have him back. I must go and thank the Rangers tomorrow. Do you know which one it was?'

Keith the accountant shook his head. 'No, but I got the impression they all knew all about him. He'd been in the Rangers' Hut scoffing digestive biscuits.'

Judy gave a watery smile.

In the distance the phone rang, and still muttering her thanks, she headed back into the sitting room where she dropped Bosun onto the sofa while she hunted for the cordless phone.

'White Oaks. Good evening.'

'Hi, Judy, it's me.'

'Oh, Jan. You okay? You sounded a bit strange earlier?'

'Yes. I'm all right. Have you got a minute or two?'

'I have. I'm just so relieved. Bosun's just turned up.'

Jan still sounded distracted. 'Gordon will be pleased. Judy, there's something I've got to tell you but before I do, please remember that I'm your best friend, we've been friends for more than twenty years and I love you a lot.'

'Blimey, Jan. You're scaring me. What is it?'

'It's Lucy. She's been here today.'

'Oh? She and that idiot Jason were here last night. They left in a bit of a rush this morning. Honestly Jan, I'm so busy, I don't know whether I'm coming or going.'

'Yes, that's the problem. Jason asked Lucy to marry him last night on the beach. She said yes.'

'What? Why didn't she tell me?'

'Because you don't like Jason and you were too busy to listen. Her words.'

Judy was silent. Stunned.

'Judy? I'm sorry. She asked me to tell you. I refused at first, but she's in such a state. This seemed the best way.'

Tears were streaming down Judy's cheeks.

'I'll have to call you back,' she sobbed and put the phone down.

She looked across at Bosun curled up on the sofa and went to the computer.

'Darling. The good news – Bosun's home and none the worse for his big adventure. But please call me when you can. Lucy's going to marry Jason. Love you. Your Jude xxx'

She pressed send and sat down to wait for the call. Lucy, her own daughter, had gone to her friend because she thought she was too busy for her. She couldn't believe it but when she thought over the last twenty-four hours she could see why Lucy felt that way. If Gordon had been here it would have been different. With two of them to split the work she could have been available to be a proper mother when she was needed. What a mess!

Six

Every Picture Tells a Story

There was real warmth in the sun as Judy strode along the seafront with Bosun trotting along beside her. The little dog had fully recovered from his adventure, although she noticed he was a bit less keen to leave her side. That was all to the good.

A red van was parked on the seafront and two men in boiler suits unloaded brightly painted panels. They were putting up the ice cream kiosk. Only a couple of weeks till Easter and Sandhaven was gradually coming to life. The sleepy winter months, when the only people about were locals, a few intrepid walkers and escapees from demanding city lives, were nearly over and soon the town would take on its Summer Season mantel. The lights would sparkle along the seafront, flags would fly in the square and old Charlie, who seemed to have been there forever, would set up his seafood shack selling wonderful crab sandwiches, cockles and pints of prawns. Gradually the town would fill until by August you couldn't move on the pavements or the beach.

Judy was looking forward to the summer season. Bookings were coming in thick and fast now and the diary was beginning to look quite full. There was still a lot to do but at least she could see that there would be money in the bank and that was reassuring.

Now all she had to do was resolve her family issues. Her daughter wasn't talking to her and even Tom, her son, had phoned last night suggesting she go to London and sort it out with Lucy.

'How can I possibly drop everything and go to London?' Judy had asked. 'None of you seem to realise that I've got a business to run single-handed down here. Dad won't be home for another three months or so and we have to make some money. This isn't some hobby or whim I've embarked on. It's real life!' And to her shame she'd burst into tears.

Tom, aged twenty and enjoying himself at University, had sounded embarrassed and muttered that he'd be down to see her soon.

'Love you, Mum, but, hey, just deal with it, will you.' He'd put down the phone.

He planned to spend most of Easter in his

student digs. He had a job in a bookshop, a neat way to get his textbooks at a discount. She had to admire his shrewdness.

'Ah, Judy!'

Her daydreams were interrupted by a cry from the other side of the road. Sharon from the Anchor Inn hailed her. She came and joined her on the sea wall.

'I'm glad I've caught you. Can you drop some brochures into the pub? It'll be easier when people ask about accommodation.'

'I will, when I've got some. Gordon was going to take some photographs and organise them, but of course that all went down the pan when he went back to sea. It's another thing on the list.'

'Okay, but now the season's starting people do come in and ask us where to stay, so I might as well send them up to you.'

Judy's mobile rang and she rummaged in her handbag. Gordon's name flashed up on the screen and Sharon mouthed good bye to her and headed off.

'Hi darling.' Gordon sounded friendly, even tender, and Judy breathed a sigh of relief. He'd been so angry when Bosun had gone missing, and then again when Judy had to tell him that Lucy was engaged to Jason. She'd wondered if they'd ever get back on an even keel. 'So, what are we going to do about Lucy?' That was better. She liked the sound of 'we'.

'Have you spoken to her?'

'I rang her mobile but it went to voice mail. I don't know if she genuinely couldn't answer or whether she just wouldn't take my call.'

'Well, if she won't talk to you, Gordon, there's nothing you can do, except perhaps send her an email congratulating her on her engagement.'

'What! To that plonker?'

'I think we might just have to accept that she's going to marry him. Tom says he's not so bad when you get used to him. He spent the weekend in London with them a few weeks ago.'

'Can't you go and see her, Jude? See if you can talk sense into her.'

'I don't see how I can go anywhere. I'm too busy with the guest house.'

'But you've got staff. Can't that Mavis run the place for a couple of days.'

Actually, that was a thought. Perhaps she could. 'I'll think about it. I wish you were here.'

'I know, sweetheart, so do I. You've got a lot on your plate and this just isn't fair.' His voice was gentle, but the signal was breaking up and suddenly the line went dead.

Thoughtfully, Judy got up and, unclipping Bosun's lead so that he could rush off to play with a poodle, she strolled along the beach. Perhaps she could go and see Lucy. There was one lady coming in tonight and staying for four or five nights. The other guests, a group of climbers, were all due to go home in the morning. She paused and punched in Jan's number. Since Lucy had gone to Jan instead of her, it made sense to ask her friend's advice.

'Good idea, Jude! Go and see her. It's a stalemate at the moment and I honestly think it's going to have to be you that makes the first move. This is supposed to be one of the happiest times in Lucy's life and at the moment she just can't enjoy it.'

Judy felt awful. 'She won't talk to me, Jan. Ask her if she'll meet me and ring me back will you? I'm going to have to make some arrangements but I think I could get away the day after tomorrow. It's a bit complicated but this mess with Lucy is more important.'

'Make sure you tell her that, won't you?'

'I will, if she'll give me the chance.'

'Jude, you ring her. I'll come if you need a

referee, but this has got to come from you.'

'Well, I'll try. I'll let you know.'

Extricating Bosun from a game of chase with the poodle that involved covering most of the passers by with a shower of sand, Judy headed back to White Oaks. She had a lot to think about.

Judy was just booking her train ticket on the internet when the bell rang and she came out to find an elderly woman in a dark anorak at Reception.

'I'm Mrs Samuels.' Her voice was low and attractive.

'Hello, I'm Judy. Welcome to White Oaks. Can you fill in a form for me and I'll get your key?'

'Sure.' Judy was beginning to notice that you could guess quite a lot about people by their writing and Mrs Samuels' was flowing and artistic.

'Single room, isn't it?'

'Yes. Am I your only guest?'

'Not tonight. I've got some climbers in, tomorrow you're by yourself but it's Sandhaven Folk Festival at the weekend, so we've got a crowd of Morris Dancers arriving.'

'That'll be colourful.'

There was a pause as Judy reached for the

key from the cupboard where they were all arranged on hooks. 'I'll take you up.'

She'd changed her mind about where to put Mrs Samuels. The top rooms were more than slightly shabby but she'd appreciate the sea view from the top floor.

'We haven't been here long,' she explained as they went upstairs, 'There's a lot of modernising to do, but we're gradually working our way round.'

Mrs Samuels walked into the room and went immediately to the window. 'It's fine,' she reassured Judy, 'and just look at that view! I'll be very cosy up here.'

Puffing gently, Mavis let herself in the back door of White Oaks Guest House.

'Hi, Mavis!' Judy was clearing up the kitchen when she arrived. 'Fancy a bacon sandwich? I've got some left over.'

'Oh, go on then.' Mavis reached for the sliced white loaf; 'the diet can start tomorrow.'

'How often do we all say that?' laughed Judy, as Kelly came through from the dining room with a tray of dirty crockery.

'What's that?' asked Kelly, loading the dishwasher.

'Diets,' explained Judy.

Kelly, who hadn't a pick on her, giggled. 'I know what you mean. My jeans were a bit tight this morning.'

Mavis snorted. 'You don't need to think about dieting, young lady.'

'Oh, I do.' Kelly was earnest in her explanation. 'I have to be really careful what I eat.'

Judy chuckled. 'I was as skinny as you when I was seventeen, Kelly. I had a twenty one inch waist when I married Gordon.'

Kelly looked disbelievingly at Judy. 'That's scary,' she announced and went back for more crockery.

'I'll give her a hand clearing tables,' Mavis donned an apron and picked up a tray.

'Before you go, I've got a favour to ask.'

'Fire away.'

'You couldn't come in tomorrow afternoon and see people in, could you?'

'Don't see why not.'

'I've got to go and see Lucy and I've got a Morris dancing group coming in for the Folk Festival this weekend.'

'Side,' said Mavis.

'Sorry?'

'Side. That's what they're called, a Morris side. My brother-in-law used to do it, although my sister said he only went along for the beer. They always seem to dance near pubs you know.'

'Morris dancers?' Kelly came in with a tray of assorted yoghurts. 'Weirdoes if you ask me. Why would a grown man go around with bells on his ankles?'

'No danger of your Matt joining a Morris side then?' Judy grinned.

'He'd be on his own pretty quick. I heard what you said. Shall I come in and help Mavis after school?'

'Well, I don't know that there's enough for two of you to do.' Judy counted the cost of two people hotel-sitting for a whole evening. 'Anyway, you wouldn't want to waste a Friday evening working, would you? Surely you'll be out enjoying yourself?'

'That's true. Matt wants us to go to the Red Lion for the darts evening.' Judy raised her eyebrows. 'I know. But they're putting on free food and if you play they give you a pint too.'

'That explains it.' Judy went on to make the necessary arrangements with Mavis and then plucked up the courage to phone Lucy. She didn't answer but Judy left a chatty message and promised to call back later to find out whether Lucy could meet her for lunch the next day. She told her she'd already booked her train ticket. It made it more difficult for Lucy to refuse her. If she headed off immediately after breakfast, she could be in London for a late lunch and she wouldn't have to rush home too early.

Judy was glad Jan had met her at Waterloo. It was ridiculous to be scared of meeting her own daughter but she knew how stubborn Lucy could be and this just had to be sorted out today. Jan treated them to a taxi to the upmarket wine bar Lucy had chosen for lunch.

Lucy had just arrived and was standing with her back to them when they walked in. Jan tapped her on the shoulder and she turned, smiled at Jan and hugged her and then turned to her mother. Instinctively Judy put her arms round her daughter, who stood stiff and unyielding, unwilling to respond. As Judy released her, though, she noticed a glittering of tears in Lucy's eyes and realised she was more vulnerable than she looked.

They sat down and ordered a bottle of wine and salads all round. The atmosphere was strained and conversation stilted.

'Right, you two.' Jan broke the ice. 'You're not going, either of you, until you're back on proper speaking terms even if we have to sit here all afternoon.'

Lucy set her jaw in a way that Judy recognised from when she was a little girl. She made a point of talking to Jan. 'I love Jason, he loves me. If my parents can't accept that it's their look out.'

Jan sat silently and looked at Judy. The couple at the table next door stopped talking and could be seen straining to hear their conversation.

'It's not that we can't accept it.' She struggled for the right words. 'Jason's not like the other men you've dated. He's very…' How could she put it without insulting him?

There was a pause as the waiter came and poured wine into their glasses and three beautiful salads, works of art on sparkling white plates, were placed in front of them.

'You think he's arrogant, don't you?'

Judy hesitated. 'Well,' she began. 'Not exactly arrogant. I'm thinking of you, Lucy…'

'That's it! You're not going to listen. You think you know best. I'm an adult, mother, I hold down a responsible job with a huge budget and I just don't need you to tell me how to live my life.' She folded her napkin, stood and reached for her jacket on the back of her chair. 'This is pointless, I'm not listening to you badmouthing the man I love.'

Jan got to her feet too. 'Lucy, this lunch is on me because I love you both. Now, as it's my treat, you'll have the good manners to stay here until we've sorted this out. Your mother is trying to understand and you going off in a huff won't help. Sit down.'

Lucy sat grudgingly and the couple at the next table put down their cutlery, waiting for the next instalment.

'When you came down after your row,' Judy reminded her daughter, 'you said he was impossible.'

'Mum, he is. But I still love him. And anyway, I don't have to justify myself to you. Or at least I shouldn't have to. I'd point out to you that Dad can have his moments.'

'That's true.' In spite of herself, Judy smiled. 'But that's him. It's different.'

'Touché, Mum. You've just shot yourself in the foot.'

Judy tried once more. 'He may not be arrogant, but you must admit Jason does have quite a high opinion of himself.'

'Yes, but then he's every right to. He's very successful and he's only done so well because he's confident. He knows what he wants and goes out to get it. You have to be like that to get anywhere these days.'

Actually, thought Judy, that was probably

true. At Barn Road School, the worst she had to deal with was petty staff room politics and Gordon's work as a Merchant Navy Officer didn't expose him to the cut and thrust of modern commerce. Maybe Lucy was right. They were a pair of dinosaurs who didn't understand.

She realised that she was going to have to concede defeat. She didn't want to lose Lucy and she knew she mustn't make her choose. There was still a problem, though. 'Maybe you're right. But you'll still have to convince your father.'

'No, I don't.' Lucy's voice was rising again. 'You do. It's his problem, not mine.'

Jan stepped in, 'I think Lucy might be right on that one, Jude. If you can accept this, it's you that's going to have to sort it out with Gordon.'

'No,' Judy wasn't accepting that responsibility, 'I don't. Jason does. I'll tell your father that I'm happy with it and then he and Jason will have to sort it out between them. I can't do any more than that.' She paused and smiled at Lucy. 'Now, show me your ring and tell me your plans.'

'We haven't really got that far. I couldn't get into it until it was okay with you. Stupid as it seems, I actually wanted to plan my wedding with my Mum.'

Jan rose and headed off to the Ladies and to settle the bill. By the time she came back, they were talking wedding dresses and venues and the couple at the next table had relaxed and resumed their own conversation.

Judy surprised herself by elbowing a young man out of the way, laying claim to a corner seat on the crowded commuter train out of Waterloo back to the South coast. She hadn't realised she could be quite so aggressive, but if you can't beat them, join them, seemed to be the only policy.

Whacked, she lay back in her seat and considered the day, ignoring the melee around her. It seemed like forever since she'd cooked breakfast for the guests this morning and left Mavis clearing up as she rushed out of the house.

She'd been gratified to find out that Lucy and Jason hadn't made any firm plans.

She closed her eyes and remembered, with a sense of rising panic, how she'd been so carried away with the warm feeling that she and Lucy were back on something approaching the same wavelength, that she'd suggested a seaside wedding in Sandhaven. Lucy had jumped at the idea.

'Oh, yes, think of the photographs. Me and Jason on a windswept headland with the ocean behind us! Wow. Great idea, Mum.'

Judy had been so pleased that she hadn't even panicked at her daughter's next words. 'You'll have finished the hotel by then, won't you? All the guests can stay with you. Perhaps we can even have the reception there, or is there a posh hotel close by? Jason and I will have to come down and do a recce.' Now, though, a reality check made her wonder if it was such a good idea. It was going to be incredibly hard work and take a lot of time she just didn't have.

The train chuntered on towards the coast as Judy wondered how to tell Gordon that she'd given the two of them her blessing, and, incidentally, that the whole hotel had to be finished quickly and to a high enough standard to host Lucy's wedding. Fortunately, they hadn't actually set any dates yet, but Judy had a feeling it would be sooner rather than later.

To her surprise, Peter from next door was sitting in her armchair, watching her television, with her dog on his lap when she walked in the door.

'What are you doing here?'

'Mavis had an emergency at home. Some plumbing disaster. So she asked me if I'd sit in here.'

'Oh.' Judy realised she'd been uncharitable but it had really irked her seeing him so at home. 'Well, thank you then. Good of you to come in at short notice.'

'Anything for you,' she thought he was joking, but she wasn't sure, 'you know that. Now, shall I get you a drink from your bar? Gin and tonic?' He rose, not waiting for her answer, and strode off into the bar, chatting as he went. 'How did it go with Lucy then?'

Judy realised she didn't want to talk about it. Not to him, anyway. 'Fine,' she said shortly. 'Actually, Peter, I'm exhausted. Skip that drink.'

'Too late!' He was relentlessly jolly as he came back carrying her gin and a pint for himself.

'Thanks. I'll head for the kitchen and set up for the morning. Did the Morris men come in okay?' She picked up her drink.

'Yes. They're quite fun. They're all down the Anchor.'

'Okay. Well, finish your programme and your pint and thanks again. I'll see you soon.'

She hoped he'd take the hint and be gone when she'd sorted out the kitchen. She clattered around, laying out the utensils she used each day, putting plates in the hot cupboard and setting her pans in place so that the morning routine ran like clockwork.

Mrs Samuels came in the front door just as Judy was checking the dining room.

'Hello. Had a nice day?'

'Mmm. Lovely. Did some walking.'

'Do you know the area?' Judy was back in hotelier mode.

'No. But it's beautiful.'

Judy realised that she wasn't as old as she looked. She wore her hair in a dated bun at the back of her head and the combination of no make-up and tired, sad eyes aged her. 'It's a pretty place. We're new to the area ourselves. Until we moved, I had no idea how spectacular the Dorset coast is.' Mrs Samuels smiled, and Judy could see what an attractive woman she'd been. 'See you in the morning, then. Good night, Mrs Samuels.'

'Eleanor.'

'Eleanor, then. Sleep well.'

Judy wondered what was behind the sadness. She was obviously on her own and she didn't seem to like it much.

Her mobile phone beeped and there was a text from Lucy.

'Hi, Mum. Spkn to Jason. Seaside wedding wd be cool. Have u spoken to Dad yet?' Nothing like piling on the pressure, thought Judy, as she went through to the sitting room and was relieved to find Bosun the only occupant of the armchair.

She decided to leave contacting Gordon till the morning and went to bed. Her window was open and she could just hear the waves swishing in and out. Sandhaven seemed a million miles from London and Judy couldn't help but be excited about the idea of the wedding, even if the practicalities seemed somewhat daunting at the moment.

The breakfast room was noisy.

At two large tables the Morris Men had all eaten full English breakfasts and were onto toast. They wore white shirts and breeches with coloured streamers sewn on. On a side table they'd placed their cocked hats and sticks which Judy thought probably had a technical name. They were a jolly lot and Judy found herself wondering what Gordon would have made of them.

Eleanor Samuels sat at a corner table, finishing her breakfast. The Morris men went off, jangling merrily, to dance in the Town Square, and while Kelly beavered away in silence, restocking the little baskets on each table with marmalade, jam and honey, Mavis wandered round collecting sugar bowls. She stopped at the corner table.

'Hello. Enjoying your stay?' Mavis was her usual blunt self.

'Yes.' Eleanor obviously hoped that this would be enough, but she didn't know Mavis.

'So, what brings you to Sandhaven? Been here before?'

The woman took a deep breath and realised, as so many people had before her, that there was no point in trying to avoid Mavis's inquisition. 'No, I wanted to come somewhere that had no memories.' There was a pause as Eleanor struggled with emotion. 'My husband died just before Christmas. I thought I was ready to come away, but now I'm not so sure. I'm not very good at being on my own,' she finished falteringly.

Mavis sat down opposite her and Eleanor struggled to fill the silence. 'So how long have you worked here?'

'Oh, only a month or so. Judy only moved in a little while ago and she needed a lot of help so she took me on as housekeeper.' Judy, coming in to pick up a jug of fruit juice, smiled. Mavis obviously felt that this was a reasonable version of events and actually was probably true. Her official title might be chambermaid, but it was clear that she intended to do the job of housekeeper. 'Her husband's in the Merchant Navy, you see, and he's been called away.'

'What did you do before that?'

'I was retired. I worked at the old Grosvenor Hotel for twenty years. Lovely old place it was, but it was big and impossible to heat. The two chaps who owned it had a job to keep up with the maintenance so in the end it was demolished and turned into flats. So, I retired, but I couldn't be doing with it. Nothing to do all day. I don't like gardening and what's the point in going for a walk unless you've got somewhere to go.'

Judy and Kelly cleared the dining room around them and the conversation paused as the phone rang.

'I'm sorry.' Judy apologised to the caller. 'I'm afraid we don't have any brochures at the moment, or a website. We've only just taken over and it's on our list of priorities. Oh, well, all right then.' Judy looked defeated.

'Lost the booking?' asked Mavis.

'Yes, I must get on about a brochure but I need photographs. Something else Gordon was going to do before he was called away.'

'My brother works for a printer.' Kelly offered. 'They do some sort of special cut price deal if you do all the artwork and preparation. They print them up on really nice glossy paper. Ever so professional, they look.'

'I'll bear that it mind, Kelly.' Judy looked troubled as she took her tray through to the kitchen.

Kelly had gone upstairs swinging a set of master keys ready to start cleaning the bedrooms before Mavis plodded back into the kitchen. Judy peeped through the window into the dining room to check that Mrs Samuels had gone. 'Been making friends?'

Mavis made herself a cup of tea and finished off her cold bacon sandwich. 'She shouldn't have come away on her own.' Mavis was dismissive, between mouthfuls. 'She's not ready yet. She might do your photographs, though. She's a photographer, or she was till her husband died. Can't get her head round it now, she says.'

Judy grinned. 'Mavis, how do you do it? You're amazing! She's been here two days and I know nothing at all about her. You meet her for ten minutes and you know her life history.'

'The poor woman didn't have much

choice,' muttered Kelly, wandering past with a pile of laundry.

There was a knock at the kitchen door.

'Sorry to disturb you,' Eleanor Samuels began falteringly, but gained confidence as Judy and Mavis smiled at her. 'I couldn't help overhearing the phone call about your brochures. If it's photographs you need, I could take some. I'm a professional photographer. It's what I do.'

'Well,' Judy was hesitant and Eleanor immediately understood the problem. 'It's okay. I need to ease myself back in – I'd do it for nothing.'

'No, no,' Judy was quick to reassure her. 'I'll pay your expenses, of course, but I couldn't run to a proper fee at the moment.'

'Don't worry about it.'

'Thank you, but there is another problem. White Oaks isn't exactly photogenic at the moment.' Judy felt disloyal to the house as she said it, but it was true.

'It is from the outside, and a bit of careful lighting can do wonders for the inside. If we only do a small print run, then as you do the place up I can come again and take some updated pictures.' Eleanor began to sound excited and enthusiastic. 'There is one other thing, though. Being a stranger here, I don't really know what to photograph. I'm not sure what the most important landmarks are.'

Before Judy could say a word, Mavis stepped in. 'We'll go out this afternoon. I'll show you all the important places in Sandhaven. The Pier, the amphitheatre, the gardens and I see they're putting the ice cream kiosk and the Punch and Judy back up again.'

Eleanor and Mavis didn't even notice that Judy had slipped away as they made their arrangements to meet at lunchtime and spend the afternoon taking some suitable shots.

At five o'clock, Judy went through to the guests' sitting room to put the gas fire on. It was chilly now and Eleanor and Mavis weren't back yet. They'd be frozen. As she stood up, she heard the front door bang and they wandered into the lounge and sank into the shabby armchairs, exhausted.

'Hi,' she perched on the arm of a sofa. 'How did you get on?'

'Great!' Mavis was enthusiastic. 'Really good. Eleanor here got some lovely shots. I reckon your brochure will be terrific if Kelly's brother can come up with the goods.'

'We're shattered! I used the digital camera so I can just email the pictures to you when I get back.' Eleanor Samuels looked as though she had enjoyed herself. Her cheeks were flushed and her eyes shone. Judy could see the kind of woman she'd been before grief had catapulted her into early old age.

'Well, when I see them I'll try and write some words and then we'll talk to Kelly's brother. What's his name, by the way?'

'Kevin,' said Mavis. 'The only thing is … she said we had to have it all set ready to print, didn't she?'

'I guess this Kevin's quite handy with a computer. I can do the basics.' Mentally, Judy added this to her list of things to do. 'But I'll have to ask Kelly if he can help us with the layout.'

'I could do that.' Mavis looked secretly pleased when Judy and Eleanor both stared at her in amazement.

'What? You could ask Kevin or you could do the work on the computer?'

'The computer. I could set it all up for you. I can do desktop publishing and all that. During that silly time when I was retired – I didn't like it, you know.'

'No,' said Judy, 'you said.'

'Well, I did a course. It was free and it was for people who didn't know how to use computers. I've got an old one that they used to have at the Grosvenor and I had so much time to practise that I was a bit of a star pupil.' It clearly never occurred to Mavis that she sounded boastful. 'I'll set up your brochure. Can I use the computer here?' Judy nodded, speechless. 'Right, well, tomorrow morning we'll put the pictures up. Judy, you can write some words to go with them and I'll dolly it all up and make it look right. Then Kevin can do his stuff and Bob's your uncle. As it were.'

After breakfast the next day Eleanor sat and waited while the dining room was cleared. Kelly was folding napkins but she kept glancing across at her. Eleanor shifted slightly in her seat, embarrassed.

'Got it!' Kelly grinned, 'I was trying to work out what was different about you. Your hair looks good like that.'

Eleanor Samuels smiled. 'I left it down. Do you think it's all right? I'm actually thinking I might have it cut short.'

Kelly stopped folding and considered her. 'Yes,' she pronounced. 'It'd suit you.'

'Jack, my husband, liked it long so I always

kept it that way. But,' she paused, 'I think it's time for a change.'

'Good for you!' Kelly said.

'Where's Mavis?'

'Out the back. I'll show you.'

They found Mavis sitting in the cubby hole that passed as an office at White Oaks. She had set up a document and started to type up the handwritten notes that Judy had cobbled together the night before.

'Ah!' Mavis was deep in concentration. 'Plug yourself in and let's download these pictures then.' They worked together quietly, each suggesting where pictures and words would compliment each other.

Judy walked past and smiled to see the two women immersed in technology. Emailing Gordon would clearly have to wait.

The peace was shattered by a sound like thunder as fourteen Morris Men clattered down the stairs in their clogs, ankles jingling and beer mugs swinging at their waists.

'Thought you lot were supposed to be light on your feet?' she joked.

'Only when we're dancing. Going to come and see us perform later?'

'I might even do that.' She grinned as she trudged upstairs to help Kelly with the rooms. Somehow, she seemed to have swapped roles with Mavis. Now how had that happened?

Seven

A Family Easter

Breakfast was going rather well. Judy had a system in place now and it ran like clockwork. The sausages and bacon, cooked earlier, sat on the top shelf of the hot cupboard with a bowl of mushrooms and a tray of tomatoes beneath them, waiting for orders to come in from the dining room. Whoever was waitressing, Mavis on this particular Thursday, made tea and toast and Judy flashed up eggs and fried bread on demand, dishing up the meals onto piping hot willow pattern plates.

Today was the calm before the storm. Tomorrow was Good Friday and the whole hotel was booked out to families. It was the first time that White Oaks Guest House had been completely full since Judy and Gordon had moved in two months before, but she knew now that it would be all right. There was still a lot of work to be done, but several people had already booked again for later in the year and that was encouraging.

'That's it. Last one.' Mavis put a piece of paper on the worktop. Judy hummed along to the radio as she expertly fried two eggs and slid them onto a plate, adding the mushrooms and tomatoes for Mavis, who re-appeared from the dining room at exactly the right moment to take it through.

In a routine now, she went to the freezer, in the depths of the walk-in larder, to take out tomorrow's sausages and was head down in the icy chamber when she heard a scream.

She banged her head on the freezer lid and let out an exclamation as she extricated herself.

'Fire! Fire!' Mavis was rooted to the spot as flames, quite high ones, leapt from the grill pan. Black smoke billowed from the cooker and began to collect at ceiling level. Judy looked around for something to put it out. She could feel the heat and the fire seemed to be taking hold. It was already difficult to see across the kitchen for smoke. Mavis stood in the doorway, screaming for help. Judy knew there should be a fire blanket, but where was it? Okay, forget that. A tea towel, there must be a tea towel somewhere? She must have forgotten to turn off the grill. The flames were getting a bit big for a mere tea towel. Judy felt the panic rising. She must do something!

There was a flurry of activity at the kitchen door as a young man with tousled brown hair, purple tee-shirt and ripped jeans erupted into the room, grabbed a tablecloth, plunged it into the sink and threw it over the grill. With a huge fizz, the flames subsided and steam mixed with the smoke. The young man turned to Judy with a big grin.

'Hi, Mum!'

'Tom!' She threw her arms round him. 'What a lovely surprise. Where did you learn to be so efficient at fire-fighting?'

'University. It happens all the time when hung-over students try to make bacon sandwiches before they're properly awake.'

Mavis found her voice. 'Well, young man. That was very impressive.'

Tom raised an eyebrow at his mother.

'Tom, meet Mavis, without whom I would probably be in a lunatic asylum by now.'

Tom put out his hand and Judy realised with a shock that her lanky teenage son had become a very good looking young man, more mature and confident than when she'd last seen him at Christmas.

'Your mother said you were working this weekend?'

'I was but another guy is going off travelling next month and he desperately needs the money. So I was noble and gave him my hours and came down to pitch in.' He gazed round the kitchen, where the fog was clearing, and the extent of the smoke damage could now be seen. 'Looks like I arrived in the nick of time.'

'This lot will take forever to wash down.' Judy looked at the blackened tiles and ceiling.

Kelly came in, taking her coat off as she walked through the door. 'What's that smell. It's disgusting, smells like... What happened here?'

'Guess!' Tom teased, grinning. 'Give you a clue. It wasn't an earthquake?'

Kelly giggled nervously. 'Yeah, okay. Something caught fire.'

'Full marks, now you've got to guess what it was. Another clue. It wasn't my mother.'

'So you're Tom. We've heard all about you.'

Tom gave a twirl, 'And do I live up to expectations?'

'Dunno yet.' Kelly was suddenly embarrassed and Judy came to the rescue.

'It'll be all hands to the pump later after the rooms are done. There's a big turn round of guests today because of Easter starting tomorrow and now we've got all this to clean.'

'Tell you what.' Tom ran a finger down the tiled wall and looked thoughtfully at the soot which came away. 'I'm going to go for a dip in the sea – it looked so inviting as the bus brought me along the front – and then I'll wash all this down for you.'

Judy looked doubtful. 'But you're here on holiday…' she began.

'I'd bite his hand off,' said Mavis. 'This needs ladders and neither Kelly nor I do heights.'

Judy laughed. 'Well, if you're sure, Tom?'

'No problems! But first, the sea calls me!'

Kelly, who'd been gazing at Tom with undisguised amazement, found her voice. 'You're not really going to swim, are you? It's freezing!'

Tom gave her a cheeky grin. 'Watch me!'

'Can't. Got to work.'

'If I come back soaking wet, will you believe me?'

'S'pose.'

'Will you rub me down with a rough towel to warm me up?' Kelly blushed and Judy stepped in.

'Tom, behave. This is Kelly who's a real

treasure. She has a boyfriend called Matt, by the way.'

Tom had the grace to look embarrassed. 'Sorry. Nice to meet you, Kelly.' He turned to his mother; 'Can I borrow Dad's trunks, Mum? Didn't think to bring any.'

'Of course.' Judy turned to her two staff. 'If you finish clearing the dining room and then head upstairs, I'll load the dishwashers while you start on the rooms.'

'If Tom's going to be here this weekend,' asked Mavis tentatively as she reached for a tray, 'would it matter if I wasn't?'

'Why?' Kelly grabbed another and a bin bag for the napkins and butter papers.

'My sister's coming to stay and it would be nice to spend some time with her but I didn't want to let you down.'

'Oh, Mavis, you should have said. Tom?' Judy looked at her son.

'Fine with me, so long as I'm paid!'

'Right,' said Judy. 'That's settled. Tom, I'll get your dad's swimmies, though I'm sure you'll end up with hypothermia.' She looked around the blackened kitchen. 'You're right, Kelly, it does smell disgusting. Open the windows, there, Tom.'

Kelly turned to her new workmate. 'Tom, do you know anything about cleaning.'

‘Not much,’ he replied cheerfully, ‘but I’ll bet you can teach me a thing or two.’

She whacked him over the head with her tray and Judy realised this was going to be an entertaining weekend.

By lunchtime, it was a lot less fun. Kelly had gone home to break it to Matt that she was working with a handsome hulk of a bloke for the rest of the weekend. Tom was up the ladder washing the ceiling and she was on her knees scrubbing cupboard doors.

‘I really am grateful, Tom,’ she said for about the tenth time.

‘Oh, knock it off, Mum. I couldn’t really just sit around and watch everyone else work. Anyway, I’ll make you pay for it another way. Can you persuade my sister that I don’t have to ponce around in a penguin suit for this wedding.’

Judy laughed, ‘Not a chance, I don’t think. She’s determined to have Jason, you and all the ushers in tail coats.’

‘I don’t know why I have to be best man anyway. Doesn’t Jason have any friends?’

‘I think it’s a nice gesture.’ She groaned as she got to her feet. ‘Of course, Jason has his own tails, but then he would.’

Tom gave her a surprised look. ‘I thought

you'd decided he was okay?'

'Well, he is, until he goes all high and mighty on us. When I said you and your father would have to hire he just said that all his friends had their own, as though we were some sort of lower life form.'

'I might buy my own, just to show him.' Tom mused. 'I'm sure I'll need tails for other do's. Quite a few of my Uni friends have them. Might be a good investment.'

Judy realised how far out of her world he was travelling. She wasn't sure if she liked it, so she changed the subject. 'As well as working with Kelly tomorrow, there's a few other jobs that require a man's touch if you don't mind. I'll pay you,' she added hurriedly.

'Sure, whatever.'

'Peter next door was going to do them, but to be honest I don't like to ask. I think he may have the wrong idea.'

'I've heard about Peter from Lucy. Sounds like he's taken quite a shine to you.'

'Hmmm. You'll be able to tell soon enough. He'll be round once he knows you're here. He's met Mum and Dad and then Lucy and Jason so once he's got to know you he'll really feel part of the clan.'

'Do you want me to talk to him?'

'No, don't be daft. I can handle it. He's just

a lonely man who needs a friend. Trouble is because your father went away when he did, he's been awfully useful. It'll sort itself out.'

'Well, when Lucy and Jason come down later, we can go and see him if you want. Put up a united front and tell it like it is.'

'Lucy and Jason?'

'Yes, they're coming down this afternoon and staying over. Didn't she tell you? She texted me the other day.'

Panic set in. 'They don't want to stay the weekend, do they? I can do tonight but after that, even you'll have to sleep on the sofa. The place is full.'

'No, they're going on to Granny's in Devon tomorrow for the weekend. Apparently Granny wants to pay for the wedding dress so Luce feels she needs to go and be nice to her and make sure that she doesn't end up with some awful crinoline.'

Judy realised how far out of the family loop she was. 'I haven't checked for texts for days. My mobile ran down and I haven't charged it up. Well, actually,' she admitted, 'I can't find the charger.'

'But what if Dad wants you?'

'I've barely been out so he can use the landline and he usually emails anyway. Mind you, I haven't picked them up for a day or two either.'

'Oh, come on, Mum, get on the case. You can't ignore us all, you know.'

'I don't want to, but you can see what it's like here.'

He came down from his ladder and put an arm round her, leaving a sooty handprint on her shoulder. 'It'll all be easier when Dad comes home.'

'I suppose so,' she agreed, though privately she wondered how that was actually going to work. She'd got very used to running her business her way. 'Let's stop for a sandwich. We're about half way through.'

She made a couple of bacon sandwiches, using the rashers left over from breakfast, and watched in amazement as Tom smothered them in ketchup.

'You don't like ketchup.'

'Times change, Mum.' It was amazing the little things she didn't know about her own family she thought, as the doorbell rang.

'Hi, Mum!' Lucy stood at the front door, stunning in a snow-white trouser suit with a scarlet camisole just showing. Jason, behind her in jeans and a designer tee shirt, was equally suave.

'Don't touch me!' squealed Judy.

'Mum?' Lucy drew back, hurt.

'Look, love! I'm covered in soot! You'd be filthy in seconds. The grill caught fire this morning and the kitchen's a terrible mess. Tom's just helping me wash everything down.'

She led them to the kitchen which still smelt faintly of burning and looked even worse with smears all over the half-washed walls.

'Hi Sis,' Tom smiled. 'Don't touch me.'

Lucy laughed. 'And I always thought we were a fairly touchy-feely family.'

Tom looked her up and down. 'Well, look at you. You're not exactly dressed for a day at the seaside, are you?'

'I'm dressed to impress Granny sufficiently for her to buy me a really nice Vera Wang dress.'

'Parasite!'

'She offered.'

'Whatever.' Tom held up his hands in surrender.

'Look, Tom, if I can borrow something to wear, I'll give you a hand while the girls talk weddings.' Jason looked around, slightly distastefully, at the mess.

'If you don't mind helping Tom, that'd be great.' Judy was truly grateful. 'I've got some details of caterers to show you and an idea for a photographer.'

'Pleasure,' his voice was slightly strained but Judy really appreciated the gesture and the effort it took.

'Right, then, come on.' She led the way through to her own ever more civilised quarters which was now bare of boxes apart from one huge one in the middle of the floor.

'What's that?' asked Lucy, desperately trying to avoid Bosun's welcoming leaps.

Judy laughed. 'It's okay, he's been in all morning. He should be clean.'

Lucy grinned as the little dog licked her nose. 'Oh, what the hell.' She turned to her mother. 'So?' she indicated the box.

'New brochures. What do you think?' She picked a sample off her desk and Lucy ran a critical eye over it.

'Great pictures.'

Judy smiled, thinking of Eleanor. Judy's brochures had coaxed her back to her camera and she was beginning work again and rebuild her business. She was also rapidly becoming a good friend.

'If you want, I'll take some of these round the local pubs and shops.' Lucy offered. 'I don't mean to be cheeky, but I might get them to take them where you wouldn't.'

Judy looked appraisingly at her daughter

and agreed wholeheartedly. 'That'd be fantastic, a real help.'

They all smiled and, at last, Judy began to feel that she had her family back.

Lucy flopped down into an armchair. 'My feet are killing me.'

Judy looked down at her strappy sandals. 'I'm not surprised in those shoes. How did you get on?'

'Fine, loads of people took them and said they'd put them on their notice boards or behind the counter for when people ask.'

'Great! Thanks.'

'It's amazing. Almost everyone knew White Oaks had changed hands and quite a few of them knew something about you – the lady with the Jack Russell Terrier or the lady whose husband had to go away, or the lady Mavis works for.'

Judy laughed. 'It's a small town.'

'I think I'd find it spooky after London.'

'It would drive me up the wall,' said Jason.

'You get used to it. Actually the Close wasn't all that different.' The cul-de-sac where the children had grown up had been a hotbed of gossip. 'Incidentally, did you know Jan and Martin are coming down tomorrow for a couple of days? Jan's been down before, of course, but Martin hasn't.'

Tom grinned. 'Don't worry, Mum, I'll give their room an extra-special dust in the morning so Martin will be impressed.'

'Thanks, you'll make a wonderful chambermaid. We'll have to get you a nice pinny.'

'If you take the mick, I'll resign,' he teased.

The 'phone rang. 'Yvonne, how lovely!'

'Yvonne from the Close?' whispered Tom. Judy nodded, listening.

'Of course. Just the two of you?' She reached for the ring binder she used as a diary. She really hoped she hadn't made any mistakes. A double booking would be a total disaster this weekend. There wasn't a spare room in town. 'A double for Tuesday and Wednesday. No problem.' She quoted a price.

There was a long pause as she listened.

'Well, I'm sorry you feel that way, but I'm running a business here and everyone has to pay. I can't let a room go for free when it could be earning me money, certainly not in the school holidays.'

Another pause.

'Well, if you change your mind, you know where we are. And I hope I'll see you when I come back to visit, though I really can't imagine when that will be at the moment.'

She clicked the phone off.

Tom looked concerned. 'You'll fall out with your friends if you treat them like that, Mum.'

'But Tom, that's how life has to be. Every time I let a room, that helps towards making this place the way we want it, not to mention feeding us and keeping you at University.'

'Still seems a bit harsh.'

Lucy looked unsure too, but Jason weighed in behind Judy. 'You're right, start as you mean to go on. People will just exploit you otherwise. It doesn't mean you like them any less, but this is business and it's hard enough to making a living. By the way, Lucy and I will pay for tonight.'

Judy laughed. 'I wouldn't hear of it, Jason, but I'm glad you understand,' she exchanged smiles with her prospective son-in-law and felt another bit of animosity fall away.

The weekend was hectic and Tom made a better handyman than chambermaid but as the rooms were full of families with small children they were messy anyway, so it didn't matter so much if things weren't perfect. Judy, however, had high standards and wasn't going to let them slip so Tom was given a hard time more than once for cutting corners.

Peter popped round with an Easter box of chocolates for Judy, but retreated when both Lucy and Tom made it clear that he had no place in the heart of the family. Judy made a mental note to go and apologise after the weekend.

Fortunately the weather was perfect so all the guests were able to head for the beach. Judy remembered from their own holidays when the children were small, that if they were happy so were the parents, so she smiled and ignored the constant drizzle of sand being walked through the house.

The bar was busy too. After the children had gone to bed, exhausted parents enjoyed coming down for a drink and meeting each other. It made for a nice atmosphere and Tom proved himself to be a talented barman and a hit with the guests.

On Easter Saturday afternoon, Tom came up with the idea of an Egg Hunt for the children on Easter Day.

'Great idea, Tom, but I've got enough to do.'

'I'll do it. It'd be fun. The kids would love

it. That little thug, Jake, in Room Three is running his parents ragged. His mum would be dead chuffed if I amused him for half an hour.'

Judy sighed. 'Oh, go on then.'

'Deal! I'll go and get some mini eggs. You make a notice on the computer and put it up in the hall,' he instructed over his shoulder as he donned his jacket and grabbed the dog lead. 'Come on, Bosun.'

'Yes, sir,' Judy muttered, smiling.

Jan found her adding the finishing touches to the poster she'd made on the computer. 'Aren't you a bit old for colouring?' she asked and Judy threw a crayon at her friend.

'Tom's doing an Easter Egg hunt for the kids tomorrow and my job was to do the poster. I've only got a black and white printer so I just thought I'd colour the chicken yellow. I might have got a bit carried away,' she conceded.

Tom rushed in with Bosun and stopped to admire her handiwork. 'Hey, Mum, that's great! The chicken looks like a canary though.'

Judy laughed. He was right. 'Well, it's what we've got. Go and put it on the notice board. You're taller than I am.'

As Jan offered to bring in fish and chips

for supper, young Jake could be heard telling Tom that Egg Hunts were for girls.

'This one isn't,' said Tom cheerfully. 'It's going to be so hard that I shouldn't think the girls will have a chance.'

'Are you only allowed to find one egg?' asked Jake.

'No. Free for all. Whoever finds them first keeps them.'

Jan and Judy exchanged glances, remembering children's parties where games had to be contrived to ensure that everyone won a prize.

'So, I could get all the eggs?' Jake checked.

'I doubt if you'd be able to find every one before anyone else.'

'Bet I could! I'm going to go and tell my sister. Bet she won't find a single one!'

Tom came back to find the two mums looking at him. 'What?'

'You're going to have a riot on your hands tomorrow,' predicted Jan.

'No, it'll be okay.'

'But what about all the children who don't find anything and start wailing?'

'Not my problem.'

'Couldn't you do it so that once they've found one egg they have to wait until everyone's found one.'

'Too tame. It'll be fine,' and off he went, whistling, to see what there was in the fridge.

Easter Sunday was one of those magical Spring mornings when there was a real promise of summer in the air. While Judy slaved in the kitchen and Kelly and Mavis rushed around the dining room serving breakfasts, Tom set up his egg hunt. There were ten children so he had twenty eggs, in the naïve belief that if he was lucky they would each find two and go away happy.

After breakfast Jake, self-appointed leader of the young hunters, gathered them all in the hall where they waited, fidgeting, for Tom to give them their instructions.

He bounced in and explained the rules, such as they were. Children scattered in all directions as their parents went to their rooms, delighted to have them occupied.

The peace and harmony didn't last long. Rosie arrived in tears with her new friend, Chloe and explained that Jake had pushed her aside so that he could get to an egg.

'He shoved me down some steps,' she sobbed.

'I'll sort him out.' Tom squatted down to talk to them. 'Have you found any eggs?' They shook their heads, sorrowfully.

'I did have one,' said Chloe, 'but that boy Aaron, took it off me.'

'But you found it. That's not fair!' Tom was indignant. 'Stay here!' He headed out to the garden where World War Three was just about to erupt.

'Okay, stop!' He roared. 'Stand still, all of you!' The chaos subsided. 'Right, how many eggs have you each got?'

'I've got thirteen,' Jake announced, spilling the eggs he'd been carrying in the front of his jumper over the table.

'I've got one.' A little girl in pink looked proud. 'I think I'm the only girl with any eggs. Aaron's got the rest.'

'Right,' Tom tried to sound authoritative. 'I think we'd better share these out a bit, don't you?' A riot broke out as the girls reached for the boys' eggs.

'You said whoever found them kept them!' Jake was not giving way.

'Well, yes,' Tom was floundering and just about to give in and apologise to the girls, when Jan came out of the hotel with a bag of Easter eggs.

'Would these help?' she asked innocently. 'Perhaps they could be consolation prizes for those who didn't find very many?'

Tom was pathetically grateful. 'Yes,' he

said meekly, 'I think it might.'

Jake and his mate Aaron looked superior as the girls queued for their eggs and rushed off, quite happy now, to tell their parents what fun they'd had.

Tom looked at Jan. 'How did you know?'

Jan laughed and glanced at Judy who was standing in the doorway. 'Put it down to twenty-plus years of parenting. Now, you look as though you could do with a strong cup of coffee.'

Tom wiped his brow. 'What I really need is a double brandy, but I'll settle for coffee.'

'Come on then,' Judy tried to put her arm around his shoulders and then realised how tall he'd got. 'Thanks, Tom, they did have a lovely time.'

'Good,' he grunted. 'Honestly, though, I don't know what these kids are going to be like when they grow up.'

Judy was at Reception seeing the last of the weekend guests out on the Tuesday morning. A few families were staying on and Jan and Martin had decided to add an extra day to their stay, but there was a big clear out today and Kelly, Tom and Mavis were upstairs stripping beds. Judy could see a mountain of washing appearing on the laundry floor.

Having Tom home had made all the difference this weekend and she realised she was going to have to take on another chambermaid. Mavis and Kelly couldn't work seven days a week and she just hadn't got time to be upstairs cleaning rooms as well as doing everything else.

A young man came in the front door, his hair long but clean and shiny. He wore a tee-shirt emblazoned with a band Judy had never heard of and the obligatory jeans and trainers.

'Hi, I'm Josh. I believe you need a chambermaid,' he blushed, 'I mean, er, chamber person.'

'I do, but how did you know?'

'I met your Tom in the pub last night and we got talking. I need a job until I go back to Uni and, if it all pans out okay, I could do the summer too.'

Judy shook her head in disbelief and laughed. 'This town is extraordinary, news travels like wildfire. Do you know Kelly?'

'My brother's in her year at school, and my Mum used to work for Mavis at the Grosvenor Hotel. Give me a go, please?'

'When can you start?'

'Now,' he grinned.

'Oh, go on then. I'll give you a trial for this

morning and then we'll see.'

'Okay, you won't regret it. Will I get paid for this morning?'

'So long as you work, yes.'

Kelly came down the stairs with a basket of clean sheets. 'Josh wants to be a chambermaid,' Judy told her.

'Cool, I've got used to working with Tom. You can take this up,' she handed him the basket, 'it's heavy.' And the two of them walked companionably upstairs.

Judy heard Tom and Josh greet each other as old friends and then her son galloped down the stairs. 'As Josh is here, I'm going to pack and get off if that's okay. It'll give me a head start. Travelling today's going to be a nightmare. I'll bet half the world's heading home after Easter.'

'Okay. Thanks for sorting out my staffing issues.'

Mavis came in from the dining room. 'Staffing issues?'

Josh strode into the kitchen, a load of laundry over his shoulder like Dick Whittington's pack, 'Where does this go?'

Tom jumped in, 'I'll show you,' and as they headed for the laundry, Mavis looked at Judy.

'What's he doing here? That's Barbara's

boy, Josh, isn't it? She used to work at the Grosvenor.'

'That's right. I've taken him on as a chambermaid, or rather chamber person, for the rest of the holidays. He can do the heavy stuff and give you and Kelly a chance to have the odd morning off.'

Mavis sniffed and her tone was disapproving, 'Whatever you say. You're the boss.'

'Mavis, Tom's been a godsend and I think a chap up there might work well. It's only for ten days and then we'll review it before the Summer.'

Josh came back through the kitchen, 'Hey, Mavis. Good to see you. Come to teach me how to clean then? My mum always said you were the best.'

As Mavis headed towards the stairs, Josh turned and winked at Judy who stifled a giggle.

After she'd put the laundry on, she went through to the office to compose an email to Gordon telling him how the weekend had gone. She wrote of the Easter Egg hunt and Jan's timely intervention and then mentioned Josh's arrival. 'It makes such a difference having someone tall and strong about the place,' she added, only thinking after she'd pressed 'send' that he might feel she was having a go at him for being away. Oh well. Not a lot she could do about it now. One day she was going to have to work out exactly what Gordon's role would be when he came back, but not now.

Mavis appeared in the kitchen to put the kettle on. 'Good idea of mine, bringing that young man in. He's a good worker and quick too. Did I tell you I'd had a word with his mother and suggested it?'

Judy stood open-mouthed at the sheer audacity of Mavis' claim, before deciding that life was too short to point out its inaccuracy.

'Thank you, Mavis,' she said meekly, 'it was a great idea,' and she went off to help Tom pack.

She stood at the door and waved to Tom as he loped off down the hill, his rucksack on his back. He'd been such fun to have around; she'd miss him. The phone rang and she ran inside to answer it, keen not to miss a single booking.

'Darling!' Oh, no, not her mother. That was all she needed. 'Lucy was telling us all about how busy you've been and how much there is still to do.'

'You can say that again.'

'Well, help is at hand. Your father and I have

cleared our diaries for next week. He's given up a golf tournament and I've cancelled my bridge afternoon. We're coming to pitch in. We'll be with you for lunch on Sunday.'

Judy's heart sank. Help and her parents didn't even figure in the same sentence.

'Um. I think we're coping actually.' Mentally, Judy ran through the list of jobs she'd planned for next week, including re-decorating two bedrooms. She tried again. 'You'll be down for the wedding, why don't you wait till then?'

'But, darling, we want to help. Till Sunday then! I'll bring my gardening gloves so you can give us the dirty jobs.' The line went dead as Judy pictured her mother's perfect manicure and immaculate clothes and looked down at her own somewhat grubby jeans.

Why hadn't she just said no? Furious, she threw the phone at the wall.

'Oh, hell,' she cried as the handset shattered into tiny pieces and Bosun ran for cover under the coffee table. Now she really was out of touch.

Eight

Lending a Hand

'Don't worry about lunch, darling. We've brought a picnic!' Judy didn't tell her mother that she hadn't even thought about food yet. Sunday morning was her busiest time of the week. Guests had to be checked out, rooms stripped, laundry done and she hoped to start decorating Room Eight this afternoon.

'A picnic?' she stared at her mother in disbelief. 'And where were you thinking we'd have this picnic?'

'Well, the beach is always so messy, sand in the sandwiches you know. But I thought perhaps that nice field at the top of the cliffs, by the lighthouse. We could stroll over there with Bosun – when you've finished work of course.'

'Mum, I won't finish work until midnight.' She pulled herself together. Her parents were staying for the week, she really couldn't fall out with them in the first ten minutes. 'It's a lovely thought, but how about if we had it here in what passes for our conservatory? Then I can keep working.'

Rose put on the hurt expression which had served her so well in getting her own way over the years, but Judy was having none of it.

'Honestly, I know you mean well, but I plan to have two bedrooms decorated by Friday and I just can't lose the time. You can help strip wallpaper this afternoon if you like.'

Judy's father came to the rescue. 'The conservatory will do fine, love, and I'll help you with the wallpaper this afternoon. Your mother can clear up after us as we go along. We came to work after all.'

Good old Dad, thought Judy. Ever the diplomat!

Mavis plodded in, duster in hand. 'The people in Room Five are just going,' she announced. 'They want to pay.'

'Money! I'm on my way!' Judy headed for Reception, 'Oh, Mavis, you've met my parents, Rose and Geoffrey, haven't you?'

'Hello again.' Mavis went straight to the point, as ever. 'So you're here to help with the decorating?'

'Thought we'd lend a hand,' trilled Rose, 'poor Judy has such a lot to do and there's just no one to support her.'

Mavis bristled. 'Well, she's got good staff and there are people in the town keen to help. Your Judy's made a lot of friends already.' She turned away. 'There's coffee in the dining room if you want some.'

'Lovely!'

She gave Rose a meaningful look. 'Give the mugs a rinse in the sink when you're done, won't you?'

Judy was perched up a ladder stripping wallpaper near the ceiling when the phone rang. It was in her pocket, sellotaped together.

She extricated it with difficulty.

'Gordon! Hang on, while I come down my ladder. Mum and Dad are here giving me a hand with the decorating.' There was a pause and then she laughed. 'You could say that!'

Smiling encouragingly at her father who seemed to have been working on his bit of wall for hours and at her mother who was washing paintwork as delicately as if it was porcelain, she went out onto the landing, carefully shutting the door behind her.

'That's better.' She sat down on the top step. 'They're driving me nuts already and they've only been here a few hours. Anyway, what's new with you?'

She listened with mixed feelings as her husband's excited voice confirmed his homecoming date.

'Mid-June, great! We'll be getting really busy so you'll be around to pitch in and help. Lucy and Jason wanted to fix their wedding for the end of June too but they were waiting to be sure you'd be home.' She wished she hadn't mentioned Jason. Her daughter's fiancé was still a sore point.

'No, it's definitely going to happen. Actually, Gordon, he's okay. He has his moments but he means well and he adores Luce. We've been getting on all right.'

Gordon obviously still wasn't sure.

'Well, none of us knows about the future. If they're happy and this is what they want to do, we have to support them.' Judy noticed that her wallpaper scraper was dripping gluey water on to the carpet and wiped it on her jeans. 'Anyway, since I foolishly agreed to hold the wedding here I haven't had too much time to worry about that side of it. The practicalities worry me far more. Making sure that the place looks as good as it can.' Gordon airily explained that once he was home everything would be fine. Judy, just about to ask him exactly how that was going to happen, bit her tongue, told him she loved him and rang off.

She went back to the scene of destruction that used to be Room Eight. 'Gordon will be home in about six weeks, so Lucy can definitely go ahead with the wedding at the end of June.'

Rose put her cloth into the bucket and rose stiffly. Judy realised with a pang that her parents were getting old. She really must be more tolerant.

'That's not long. Lucy has some very smart ideas for this wedding. You know we've ordered the dress?'

'Yes, I meant to talk to you about that,' Judy resumed her position at the top of the ladder. 'It must be costing a fortune.'

Rose leant against the wall her husband had just stripped and squealed as her sleeve got wet. 'Well,' she began. 'It was a lot but Lucy knew exactly what she wanted and...'

Geoffrey intervened, 'We're happy to do it, love. We think the world of Lucy and Tom. You know that.'

Rose went on. 'Anyway, with all the other things she wants. The flowers flown in from Jersey and that photographer from Chelsea, it's the least we can do.'

Judy, who'd heard nothing about the

flowers or the photographer and had, in fact, been asking around locally to see who was good, decided to keep her counsel.

The phone rang again and then stopped. She took it from her pocket to find that the sellotape had come loose. Why had she been so childish and thrown it at the wall? She looked at her mother's attempts at washing paintwork and decided that her fury had been entirely justified. She tightened the tape and it rang again.

She laughed. 'Okay, Josh, what did you forget?'

She listened, smiling, as her new chambermaid, or chamberperson, explained that he'd accidentally taken the master keys home but would keep them safe and bring them back in the morning. 'That's really a sacking offence, but I'll let you off this once. Do you mind bringing them round now though? I really don't like having them off the premises.'

'Yes, okay.'

'Just come up. I'm decorating in Room Eight.'

They worked on in companionable silence and it was only a few minutes before the door flew open and Josh erupted into the room brandishing the keys.

'Wow, doesn't take long to wreck a place,' he commented helpfully.

'Thanks. I'd noticed.' Judy looked down on him from her perch. 'Josh did you meet my parents this morning? Geoffrey and Rose, Josh, our new chambermaid.'

Geoffrey held out his hand, covered in wet wallpaper, and Josh to his credit shook it. Rose looked him up and down. 'Well,' she said, eventually, 'chambermaids never used to look like you, I must say.'

Josh laughed easily. 'I think we'll have to invent a new title. Domestic operative might fit the bill.' He was long and lanky and never appeared to hurry, but he zipped through the work and was already a feature of White Oaks. Judy would miss him when he went back to University. 'Do you want a hand?'

Tempting though it was, Judy declined the offer. 'No, we'll manage. You did your bit making beds this morning.'

'Actually,' Josh looked thoughtfully round the room. 'I've got some mates home from Uni. Would you like us to come and blitz it? We'd have it done in a couple of days.'

'Have you ever decorated before?' asked Geoffrey.

'Yes,' Josh sat down on the windowsill that Rose had just washed, 'oh, yes, lots of times.'

‘I’m sure we can manage with the three of us, a family effort, you know.’ Rose sounded superior and dismissive.

Judy’s hackles rose. ‘Actually, Josh. That would be great. If you could get together a few friends and come in that would be brilliant. Kelly’s back at school, but Mavis can do the rooms on her own, so you could concentrate on this. I want to get room nine done this week too if we can.’

‘Okay. See you in the morning then. Same rate as when I’m cleaning?’ he checked with Judy.

‘Yes, but you have to work,’ she warned.

‘’Course. You can rely on me.’ And he was gone.

Josh was super-enthusiastic, rather like an over-zealous Labrador puppy, and as he shut the door the room seemed quiet and empty.

‘Well, so what are we going to do for the week now then?’ Rose’s tone was brittle.

‘Oh, Mum. It’s nothing personal. There’s so much to do here I promise you won’t be idle. But, if I can get a gang of youngsters on the job it will be quicker than us struggling with it. Now let’s just finish these bits and go downstairs and have a glass of wine with the News.’

‘We met your nice neighbour, Peter, when we were down last time. Why don’t we invite him in for a drink?’

‘Maybe later in the week. He’s away till tonight.’

‘What a shame! He was such a gentleman.’

Judy reminded herself that she had to go and see Peter. When he’d come round to bring her Easter chocolates her children had made it very clear that he was not welcome. She needed to apologise and clear the air. He’d been such a help, perhaps too much so, but she must make sure they were on an appropriate footing before Gordon came home.

The next morning White Oaks Guest House felt like a set from a television makeover show. There were people everywhere.

Josh arrived with four friends. He introduced them to Judy, but she was never quite sure which was which. There was one they called Oz (she didn’t know why) who had a purple woolly hat, which he never shed, but the others were indistinguishable, shaggy and uncoordinated. However, they were energetic and bounded around enthusiastically which made her feel she’d get her money’s worth.

Judy had found her mother a job mending the pillowcases and duvet covers which had split along the seams. This was actually a useful occupation, something that Judy kept meaning to do. Her father, however, was at a bit of a loose end.

Mavis found him reading the paper. 'The devil makes work for idle hands,' she'd said briskly and thrust a duster at him. 'You can give me a hand. The dresser in the dining room needs a good polish.'

'I don't really do dusting,' Geoffrey began, 'I'm more a gardening sort of person really.'

'Hmm.' Mavis was unimpressed. 'Well, it's the dusting that needs doing and it's raining outside.'

Judy grinned and decided to keep out of the way. She remembered her determination to clear the air with Peter next door and, as everyone else was fully occupied, this seemed a good moment to pop round and see him.

She found him attempting a crossword at his kitchen table.

'Ah,' he rose to greet her with a kiss. 'What a nice surprise. It's usually me popping in on you. Coffee or are you in your usual rush?'

Judy was determined that she shouldn't

hurry this. He was such a nice man and had been so kind, but she had to make sure that he understood the situation before Gordon came home. 'Coffee would be lovely. There are people working all over my house so I thought I might as well come and see you.' She cleared her throat. 'I wanted to have a chat.'

He paused, spoon poised over a cafetiere. 'No need, my dear. Your friend made the position perfectly clear.'

'What?'

'Your friend, Jan. She came to see me, now when was it? Must have been the Tuesday after the Easter weekend.'

Judy was nonplussed. 'What did she say?'

'Well, you probably know that. I presume you sent her.' He poured the coffee and handed her a mug. 'And with Lucy and Tom coming to see me as well I think I've got the message.' He looked embarrassed.

Judy took a sip of her coffee, which was much too hot but she barely noticed. 'Peter, I know nothing about this. What exactly did all these people say to you?'

Judy's mobile, always in her pocket, rang. It was Josh to let her know that the boys had stripped both rooms and were ready for her instructions.

'Both rooms?' she cried. 'But we were going to do one at a time.'

She listened for a minute. 'No, no, no! Stop! You are not to start a third one. These rooms all have to be ready for the weekend. You've what? Do nothing else until I get back. None of you!'

She put down her coffee and jumped to her feet. 'Sorry, Peter. This'll have to wait. If I'm going to have a hotel left I must go and see what these students have done. Can I come back and finish my coffee later?'

Peter smiled sadly. 'Whenever, Judy.'

She grinned awkwardly as she ran from the back door. 'See you later. I will be back.'

The scene of devastation that used to be the top floor of her hotel appalled her. 'Josh we were going to do one room at a time. That way there's only one out of commission and I can let the others.'

'Um, actually, it's not just the two. While I was on the phone to you Oz and the others started on the third one. We might as well finish stripping it now.'

'So, you're telling me that you've destroyed three rooms.'

'Well, yes. But we'll start painting soon and they'll be back together again before you know it.'

'Josh, be realistic. They won't.' She looked him in the eye. 'I know you like the destructive bit, but I want total honesty now. Has any of you ever decorated before?'

There was a long pause. 'Not actually a whole room, no.' Josh had the grace to look ashamed. 'But we've all helped. You know, our dads and things.'

'Right. Now we know where we stand.'

Mavis clumped up the stairs. 'Your dad's a natural. He's made a lovely job of the dresser and now he's started on the hall table.'

Judy gave a weak smile. 'You're a wonder, Mavis. I can't ever remember seeing him with a duster in his hand in all my forty odd years.'

'He's enjoying it. He's been telling me about the goings on at that Golf Club of his. It's a wonder your Mum lets him go. What's happening up here?'

'Josh and the boys have been a bit over-enthusiastic. While I was next door, they got carried away and stripped eight, nine and ten.'

'Well, they need doing.'

'I don't think you understand, Mavis. This lot,' she waved a hand at Josh and his mates, who stood around, shamefaced, 'go back to University at the end of the week and I've let all the rooms for Friday night.'

'Jim,' said Mavis.

'Gym?'

'You need Jim.'

'Mavis, I think I've got enough to do without joining the gym.' Judy wondered where this conversation was going.

'No, not gym. Jim.' Mavis spoke as though dealing with a small child. 'Jim did all the decorating at the Grosvenor when I worked there. He's retired, but he'd come in and help you out. He'll do anything for me.' Judy didn't ask why. 'He'll supervise this lot too and your father can lend a hand. You'll get your rooms done. I'll go and ring him.'

'Um … OK.' As so often happened Judy felt events overtaking her, but something had to be done.

Moments later, her father appeared with some black sacks. He ignored Judy. 'Right, you lot. Mavis tells me we've got a bit of an emergency up here. Let's get cleared up first.' He peered into each of the three rooms and picked two students at random. 'Get all this wallpaper off the floor in these rooms. You two finish stripping the wallpaper in room ten.' He turned to Judy as the students went back to work. 'My old Chief Executive skills haven't left me completely,' he said proudly. 'Now, Mavis is phoning her friend, Jim. You go and do whatever you need to do and I'll stay up here and keep this lot at it.'

'Thanks, Dad.'

Meekly, Judy ran downstairs and was just emptying a dishwasher when she remembered what Peter said. What had Jan and her family been up to going behind her back? She really must sort this out.

She was just about to go next door when the doorbell rang. Oh, no, not guests. This really, really wasn't the moment.

On the doorstep was a smiley elderly man in a stripey jumper. 'Jim, at your service,' he said. 'Mavis called me.'

'Blimey that was quick!'

'I only live round the corner. Now where do I go?'

'Hello, Jim.' Mavis appeared from nowhere.

'Ah, Mavis, love. Where's the damage then?'

'I'll take you up to the top floor. You've got plenty of help. Judy's father, Geoffrey, is a real treasure. He can be your second-in-command.'

Jim looked over his shoulder at Judy.

'Don't you worry, we'll have all this fixed in no time and I won't rip you off.'

'I'll be up in a minute,' promised Judy as a smart woman in a bright red jacket appeared on the path. 'Can I help you?'

'I'm Liz Marshall. Cambridge Hotel. Just behind the seafront. I'm the membership secretary of the local Hoteliers' Association. We've been terribly remiss. I should have been round to see you weeks ago. Can I come in and have a quick word.' She strolled past Judy into the hall. 'Oh, you have improved things. It was always so dingy in here.'

'Actually all I've done is changed the lights,' Judy was pleased. 'It makes a difference though.'

'It all smells so fresh too. It was a bit grubby, wasn't it?'

'Grubby! It was filthy,' laughed Judy, immediately warming to this woman. 'Coffee?'

'Love one, but not if I'm stopping you.'

'With the chaos that's here this morning, I don't think it'll make any difference. Come through.'

Judy led Liz through to her own quarters where Bosun gave the new visitor a good checking over and Rose looked up from her mending.

Judy introduced them. Her mother volunteered to make the coffee and disappeared off to the kitchen.

'So,' said Liz, settling onto the sofa with Bosun, 'how's it been going?'

Where to start?

'Well, apart from the conservatory roof,' she indicated a blue tarpaulin still in place from where Peter had fallen through months before, 'ten rooms to decorate, my husband being called back to sea and my daughter getting married here in six weeks time, it's been a doddle. And that's without all the little day to day problems.'

Liz laughed. 'Sounds like the life of an average hotelier. Was that Jim Foster I saw coming in?'

'Yes, he's come in to lend a hand. We've got a bit of a decorating crisis upstairs.'

'He'll sort you out. Jim's great. And you've got Mavis working for you, haven't you?' The Sandhaven grapevine didn't surprise Judy any more.

'Without Mavis, I'd be insane by now. She's great. Formidable, but I couldn't have managed without her.'

There was a knock and Rose appeared, wearing Mavis' pinny which was about five sizes too big for her. Judy almost expected her to curtsey.

'Coffee?' she poured for them. 'If there's anything else, just let me know.'

Liz grinned. 'Well, now. Are you going to join the Association? We have a dinner dance once a year and several social events and meetings. It'll be a good way to meet people.'

'Yes, why not.' Judy produced her cheque book from the desk. 'Frankly, I've spent so much over the last couple of months an extra few quid is neither here nor there.'

'Don't worry. You'll be packed out all summer. Just wait and see.' Liz's confidence was reassuring and a chat comparing notes about guests and the things that happen to hoteliers left Judy feeling better.

Liz rose to go and Judy thanked her. 'It's been good to talk. Come again.'

'No, come and see our place. Just give me a call and when you're down the town come in for coffee.' She gave her a card. 'And if you've got any problems I might be able to help with, pick up the phone.'

'Don't say that, you'll hear from me a dozen times a day.'

Liz laughed. 'Looks to me as though you've got it all under control.'

Judy closed the door and, with a warm

glow of belonging, went to find her mother in the kitchen. Rose was carefully washing the coffee cups.

'Nice woman. Smart. She'd be a nice friend for you, dear.'

'Yes, Mum,' said Judy, feeling about six, and ran upstairs to see how the decorating debacle was progressing.

She paused on the stairs as she heard Jim issuing instructions. 'And,' he concluded, 'Just because we're going to do this job quickly I don't want anyone cutting corners. I've been painting and decorating for over forty years and I'll know.'

Judy tiptoed back downstairs. It was clearly best for her to keep out of the way.

Peter was still struggling with his crossword when she tapped on his back door. He beckoned her in. 'I didn't think you'd come back.'

'As ever, it's a bit of a mad house next door.' She accepted a cup of coffee and leant back in her chair. This wasn't going to be easy.

'So, I presume my friends and family have, in effect, warned you off? By the way, I will be having strong words with them all for going behind my back.'

Peter looked embarrassed at her directness. 'Well, in a manner of speaking, yes. But, Judy, I never really thought anything else. If you weren't happily married, I'd have loved to have…' He struggled for the words.

'But I am,' she said gently.

'I know. I've seen the look on your face when you answer the phone and it's Gordon.'

'But that doesn't mean we can't be friends.'

'No.' He paused. 'I thought it did. I wasn't sure I could cope with being around you on those terms, silly at my age I know, but Jan said you were the best friend in the world and I shouldn't miss out.'

Judy laughed. 'We go back a long way.' She wondered if this was a step too far, but she had to give it a go, 'Peter, you don't have to be on your own, you know.'

'Well, actually,' he looked away and indicated a pile of scrap paper next to the newspaper. 'If we're going to be just friends, do you think you could help me with something?'

Judy raised a questioning brow.

'I thought I might try internet dating, but I've got to come up with a personal profile. I'm not sure what to put.'

'Peter, I'd love to help. I really can't stop now, but bring round what you've come up with this afternoon and we'll have a cup of tea and see how it looks.' She rose and he quickly moved to open the back door for her. She kissed him on the cheek. ''Bye, my friend. See you later,' and, breathing a sigh of relief, she popped next door with a light step. She needed a friend; she didn't need a suitor. But just wait till she got her hands on Jan and her children. How dare they!

By Thursday morning, Judy was amazed at the progress that had been made. The top rooms were all painted and the wallpapering was nearly complete. What's more, the students had learned how to do the job properly. Jim had proved an absolute godsend, not only did he know what he was doing he was able to teach the lads but still let them have fun.

'He's a star, Mavis. Thank you so much.' Jim had agreed to carry on and keep working his way round the rooms. He promised to stay at least until the wedding and with his help, Judy began to feel confident that the place might be ready.

She was sitting drinking coffee with Peter putting the final touches to his internet profile. He'd made himself sound like a bit of an old buffer but, with Judy's help, he now came over as the gentle funny man he really was.

The bell rang. 'That'll be Mr and Mrs Richards checking out. They've been visiting their daughter and her husband.'

She went out to Reception and, as she took their money, they told her what a nice time they'd had.

'It's lovely here. Really cosy. Such a shame you're closing.'

Judy started. 'What?'

'When we were booking, we spoke to another hotel and they said you were closing down.'

'Closing down! I've only just opened.'

'Oh,' Mrs Richards looked confused. 'Well, they were quite clear.'

'Do you know who you spoke to?'

'I'm not sure.' She was vague and Judy realised she didn't want to cause trouble.

'Not to worry. It must be a misunderstanding.'

Preoccupied, she wished them a good journey home and went back to Peter.

'Bear with me, Peter. I must just make a phone call.' She picked up Liz's card. Someone from the Hoteliers' Association needed to know about this.

To her amazement, Liz laughed when she told her what had happened. 'Be flattered, Judy. All it means is that you're doing well and someone thinks you're a threat. I've a shrewd suspicion who it might be, he's played some dirty tricks before, but don't worry. It shows you're beginning to be successful.'

Judy relaxed. It was true, a trouble shared and all that. She felt better already.

'By the way,' Liz continued, 'are you full this weekend?'

'Yes.'

'Good. I was talking to the Tourist Information Centre this morning and apparently there isn't a spare bed in the town already. It must be something to do with the mediaeval jousting festival in Corfe Castle.'

Judy glowed with pride. 'No, I've got no space.'

'Okay. Best get on then. See you soon.'

Peter grinned at her. 'Sign of success when people try to sabotage you?'

'Apparently.' Judy sat back down. 'Leaves a nasty taste though.'

'That's business. I'll leave you in peace. When do your parents leave?'

'Early afternoon. Actually, it hasn't been

too bad, but it's definitely long enough. Why don't you join us for lunch?' On their new-found friendship footing she could invite him without weighing up what he would think and how it would look.

'Nice idea, but I'll leave you to it. I'll pop back and say good bye to them later, though.'

The students pitched in helping Rose and Geoffrey take their luggage to the car. Judy wasn't entirely sure whether it was out of the goodness of their hearts or their eagerness to see them on their way. Mavis had put Geoffrey on the cleaning rota and he'd proved to be a good chambermaid, but Rose had been more difficult to occupy. She'd decided to keep them in treats and her fairy cakes had become legendary. The students could regularly be heard mimicking, 'just like I make for the WI' in a high pitched and very accurate take-off of Rose's cultured whine.

It was only a few minutes before the first guests of the weekend arrived and Judy was kept busy showing people in and generally making sure everyone was happy.

One of the rooms on the top floor was not quite finished when the last couple arrived. Judy sat them in the lounge and went upstairs. Josh was balanced on a ladder, hanging curtains, Jim was fitting the door handles and Oz and another one, who seemed to be called Tree, were making the bed.

She went downstairs. 'Your room's not quite ready,' she said with masterly understatement. 'I'll store your luggage but could you come back in a couple of hours.'

The woman turned to her husband. 'That'd be fine, wouldn't it, dear? Gives me a chance to look round the shops. There's a lovely candle shop at the bottom of the hill.'

The husband looked resigned. 'Yes, dear.' He rose stiffly. 'No problem, we'll be back later, a little lighter in the wallet no doubt.'

Judy smiled her thanks and went back to the top floor where order was rapidly being restored.

'When you've done that there's a beer each in the bar for you.' She told the students. 'You've done a really good job this week. We'd never have achieved all this without you.' She looked at Jim for corroboration.

Grudgingly, Jim concurred. 'You've done a grand job, lads. And you know how to do it properly now, don't you?'

'Right,' Judy interrupted. 'I'll just put the hoover round in here and then someone who's feeling strong can bring Mr and Mrs

Price's luggage up.' She sniffed. 'I hope they don't mind the smell of new paint.'

The students were all gathered in the bar having a beer with Jim, and Judy was enjoying her role as barmaid, when the bell went at Reception.

All the weekend guests were in and, with satisfaction, she'd turned the sign round to 'No Vacancies'.

A family of four stood in the hall, surrounded by luggage. 'Hello,' the father boomed, holding out his hand. 'We're the Appletons. Phoned earlier in the week. Family room for the weekend.'

Judy felt the blood drain from her face and her heart started to pound. She remembered the call. She'd been right in the middle of deciding on a paint colour with her mother and she hadn't written the booking down. An absolutely fundamental mistake. How could she have been so stupid?

She found her voice, though it came out croaky. 'Come and sit down while I just check the diary. Leave your luggage there.' She showed them into the lounge. 'I won't keep you a minute.'

'Is there a problem?' Mrs Appleton looked concerned.

'Um. Just bear with me a moment.'

She bolted for her own quarters and looked at the diary, though she knew what was there. All rooms taken and a family of four who she knew had booked. Liz's words rang in her ears. 'There isn't a bed to be had in the town this weekend.'

What on earth was she going to do now?

Nine

Home is the Sailor

It was sweltering hot. Now, Judy knew what Liz Marshall, Secretary of the Hoteliers' Association, had meant when she promised that White Oaks would be full every night. She was run off her feet and loving every second of it. With Lucy's wedding a mere two weeks away and Gordon due home next Thursday she didn't have a second to herself, but, thanks to Jim the decorator's intervention, the hotel was looking good and business was certainly brisk.

The phone rang. It was Kelly. 'I spent too long on the beach yesterday and I've got heat-stroke,' she whimpered. 'I don't think I can come in today.'

Judy made sympathetic noises, only pointing out gently that the hotel was full and she'd been relying on her. 'Don't worry, Mavis and I will do it. Hope you feel better soon. See you tomorrow.'

The guests divided into two camps. There

were those whose clothes had become skimpier as the week progressed and who thought the weather was wonderful. The others were the complainers who'd come away in June to avoid the heat of August and felt that the elements were waging a personal vendetta against them by bringing summer early. Mr and Mrs Jackson fell into the latter category. Well, no. Actually, no one knew what Mr Jackson thought as it seemed he was not allowed to speak other than to agree with his wife. Judy could hear her holding court in the breakfast room.

'Really, you know, they should think about air conditioning. The rooms are far too hot to sleep.' Mavis, who was always on Judy's side, answered but as the fried bread sizzled, Judy couldn't hear the reply.

Mavis stomped through the swing door, her tray laden with finished breakfast plates. Empty plates meant happy guests, thought Judy with satisfaction.

'Stupid woman.' Mavis grunted as she bent over to load the dishwasher.

'Who?' Judy didn't really need to ask.

'Mrs J. Air conditioning, indeed! I told her it was an Edwardian house and she should be thankful the windows opened at all.'

'Thanks, Mavis.'

Mavis shook her head. 'Honestly, she's never satisfied, that one. Don't know why that nice man puts up with her. Nothing's ever good enough for her.'

Judy grinned. She may have only had White Oaks for a few months, but she'd soon learnt that there were some customers who were determined to find fault.

She placed a sausage on each plate with a flourish and looked at the breakfasts with satisfaction. She thought with secret glee how surprised Gordon would be when he came back. There was still a lot to be done to the building but the business was definitely on its feet.

The phone rang and Judy wiped her hands to write down a booking. Since the disaster a month or so ago when she'd forgotten to make an entry in the diary, she was scrupulously careful. It was only thanks to Liz that a total disaster had been avoided. She'd called in a favour and The Appleton family had finally been put up, at Judy's expense, at a spectacularly posh hotel along the coast. It had been a very expensive mistake and one that Judy would be sure never to make again.

Mavis trudged back out to the kitchen as Kelly crept in the back door.

'I didn't want to let you down.' Judy looked up. Kelly's usually bright eyes were red and swollen and she was pale and drawn. Definitely not sunstroke then. Knowing Kelly, it wouldn't be long till she spilt the beans.

'Thanks for coming in,' Judy was truly grateful. 'Do you want to talk about it?'

Kelly shook her head silently. 'I'll only cry again.'

Mavis, never one to be diplomatic, came in with a tray. 'That Matt playing you up, is he love? Told you he was too good looking by half.'

A half-strangled sob escaped and Kelly headed for the stairs with a basket full of clean laundry.

'What did I say?'

'I think she's at what one would call "a difficult age". Don't you remember, Mavis? Everything matters so much when you're seventeen.'

'It was different in my day. You just got on with it.'

'You were a child of the 'sixties, though, weren't you? Free love and all that?'

'For some maybe. I was courting my Frank and he didn't go in for that sort of stuff.' Mavis sniffed. 'I'd better go and see what's the matter with her.'

'I'll go.' Judy jumped in quickly. Mavis seemed to have done enough harm already.

Loud sobs could be heard coming from the linen cupboard as Judy ran upstairs. She opened the door. The towels Kelly was putting away would be wet again at this rate.

'Kelly. What's happened?'

'It's Matt. I'm really sorry I'm in such a state. I don't know what to do.'

'What's happened? Has he...?' Judy searched for the up-to-date word. 'Dumped you?'

'No, he loves me. He said so.'

'So...?'

'He's got a chance to go to the Red Sea for six months as a dive instructor.'

'Wow! What a wonderful opportunity.'

'Yes, but six whole months and he'll go at the end of next week! What am I going to do?'

Judy bit her tongue. She was not the right person to ask. Gordon had been in the Merchant Navy when they'd met and they had been apart for a large proportion of their marriage. 'It's not always easy, but you can't stand in his way. He'll regret it forever if he doesn't go and he might blame you.'

'I know. But what if he doesn't come back, or meets someone else?'

Judy was saved from answering by the phone ringing downstairs. She ran to get it, smiling at the Jacksons who stood on the landing, coats neatly folded over their arms, ready to go out.

Lucy was on the phone confirming that she would be down the following Wednesday, just to do a few errands before the wedding ten days later. Judy stopped listening as her daughter reeled off a list of things she still had to do. 'And the photographer's going to 'phone you to confirm what time he's arriving. He'll be down on Friday to get some casual shots before the day itself.'

Judy was stuck for words. This was all getting out of hand. No one's photographer arrived the day before a wedding.

'Oh, and the flowers. The lilies are being flown in from Jersey and the florist from Bournemouth will be at the hotel about seven o'clock on the Saturday morning.'

Judy decided she had enough to think about at the moment and, since Lucy seemed to have everything under control, she would just keep out of it for now. Currently her main problem was that she'd lost so much weight that the smart and very expensive suit she'd bought to wear was now too loose.

'Lucy. Is there anything you actually need me to do between now and when you come down?' she asked. That was all she really needed to know. Having ascertained that there wasn't, she told Lucy how much she was looking forward to it all and rang off.

Mavis and Judy worked downstairs all morning, while Kelly did the rooms. It seemed best to keep them apart. Mavis' blunt speaking wouldn't help this morning.

It was nearly lunchtime when the Jacksons came back from the town. Judy was just checking in Mr Payne, a serious looking man in a tweed jacket. He wore glasses and carried a laptop and asked numerous questions. Where should he go for dinner, could she recommend any walks, was there any chance of an early breakfast? Judy branded him a nuisance and decided his name was appropriate.

She showed him into a nice room with a sea view and turned to greet the Jacksons.

'Had a nice morning?'

Mr Jackson nodded. 'We've been to the market.'

'Oh, yes. What did you think of it?' Judy regretted the question as soon as she'd asked it.

'There was quite a lot there…' Mr Jackson began.

'Lot of tat, though,' his wife interrupted, 'and the Farmers Market was pathetic. A few bits of cheese and some organic meat that looked as though it had been lying around for a while.'

'It's very popular.' Judy ventured.

'Well, I suppose some folk have nothing better to do. We're going to Weymouth this afternoon. There's a shop there that does hand made soaps. I like to give them as Christmas presents.' Judy hid a smile. It was only June!

They went upstairs and Judy heard the clank of Kelly's master keys as she locked the linen cupboard. She must have finished work.

'Ah, young lady.' Judy held her breath. What was Mrs Jackson going to complain about now? 'Could we have a couple of extra tea bags please and some more sugars?'

'Of course.' Judy heard Kelly unlocking the cupboard again.

'I overheard you talking about your young man this morning.'

'Oh, sorry.'

'I've got some advice for you. Ken here was in oil.' Judy banished the vision of Ken swimming about in some viscous liquid. 'He travelled all over the world.'

Judy moved to the bottom of the stairs, ready to interrupt if necessary. There was a silence.

'We're still together,' Mrs Jackson went on, 'and do you know why?'

Another silence. Kelly wasn't exactly contributing to this conversation.

'I'll tell you. Because I just let him go. Wished him well, waved him off and got on with my own life.'

Mavis had joined Judy at the foot of the stairs. 'I should think he was thankful to get away,' she whispered. Judy put her finger to her lips.

'The secret,' she continued, 'is to ensure that they always want to come home. Make yourself irresistible.' Mavis and Judy exchanged glances. Mrs Jackson? Irresistible? Surely not. 'Stop moping around, smarten yourself up. Have your hair done and put some make up on.'

Kelly's voice sounded small. 'You're probably right.'

'Stop drooping child. Put your shoulders back, hold your head high and smile.'

'But…'

Mrs Jackson became brisk. 'But nothing!

Give him his head; let him go and he'll come back. Won't he, Ken?'

Judy peered up the stairs. Ken was nodding.

'Anyway, we're going for a cup of tea. Come on, Ken.' They headed for their room and Kelly locked the cupboard again and was waylaid by the man in the tie.

'I wonder if I could ask you a couple of questions?'

Judy couldn't hear what was going on.

'I reckon he might be a journalist,' she whispered to Mavis, but she shook her head.

'No, he's worse than that. I'll bet he's a hotel inspector.

Judy's heart plummeted. Kelly sobbing away upstairs, the Jacksons who moaned about everything. This was not what she wanted the inspector to see.

'What makes you think so?'

'The kind of questions he asks. And he's got a laptop with him.'

'People do carry laptops, Mavis.' Judy was still not sure.

'Not in Sandhaven they don't. He's not on holiday. I'll find out. He's coming downstairs now.'

'Hello.' Mavis was at the bottom of the stairs. 'So, what brings you to Sandhaven?'

The man paused, unable to go any further as Mavis blocked the way. 'I'm – er – here on business.'

'Not many people come here on business. Need any directions?' This was Mavis trying to be subtle.

'I'm going to the Tourist Information Centre.'

'Down to the beach and it's just opposite the stone jetty.'

'Thanks for your help.' Mavis watched through the window as he stopped outside and wrote something in a notebook. She was triumphant.

'He might be a journalist,' Judy proffered, 'writing a piece on the area.'

'Hmm. Well, we'll see. You just mark my words.'

Kelly came downstairs. 'I reckon that man's a reporter.' She said. 'He asked me loads of questions about the hotel and what it was like to work here.'

'What did you say?'

Kelly gave a watery grin. 'I said it was great and all our guests loved it. All right?'

Judy smiled. 'And Mrs Jackson's got a new job as agony aunt?'

'Would you believe it?' said Mavis, 'I can't believe that woman has the nerve to give anyone advice. The man's a poodle for heaven's sake.'

'He might not be, you know.' Judy kept her voice low. 'He might have learned how to make it work. Perhaps he doesn't mind.'

'Or perhaps,' Kelly seemed to have perked up, 'he's a real stallion in the bedroom and gets his kicks that way.'

'Kelly!' Judy and Mavis both looked shocked.

'Honestly,' Mavis recovered first. 'That imagination of yours will get you into trouble one day.'

Kelly sniffed, grinned and went to hang up the master keys.

'Will you be all right for breakfast tomorrow?' checked Judy. 'If you're well enough that is.'

Kelly had the grace to blush. 'I'll be here.'

The day was hotter than ever and Judy wondered if a literal interpretation of The Naked Chef would be acceptable. Probably not, she thought, as she opened the back door and all the windows in the kitchen. Kelly arrived early, breezing in and hanging up her coat and backpack.

Judy glanced at her, and then looked again properly.

'Hey, Kelly, you look great. Like the hair!'

'My friend Laura did it, she's a hairdresser, and, look, Sarah did my nails,' she showed off a perfect manicure. 'I thought about what Mrs Jackson said, and I reckon she's right. I want Matt to remember me like this while he's away. And I've been and found out about flights. If you can give me some extra hours I should be able to go and see him at the end of the summer.'

Judy smiled. 'I'll see what I can do.'

Mr Payne was first into breakfast, followed almost immediately by the Jacksons. He ordered scrambled eggs and sat watching as Kelly served the Jacksons.

Judy listened at the door as Kelly took them their tea.

'Well, you look very nice. That young man will certainly sit up and take notice, won't he, Ken? We'll just have a poached egg each today, something light as we have the journey home.'

Kelly wafted back into the kitchen, walking tall, radiant from Mrs Jackson's compliment.

'She's right,' she told Judy, 'my Matt was all over me last night.'

Judy mentally trawled through her wardrobe. Jeans, now too big for her, tee shirts and sweatshirts, a few boring straight skirts and blouses from her old job. Nothing to set the world on fire.

'Might be an idea to keep the personal stuff off-limits,' she suggested tartly. 'If Mr Payne is an inspector he doesn't need to know all about your love life.'

Kelly, rebuffed, busied herself making toast and Judy felt mean.

The Jacksons checked out on the dot of ten o'clock. As Judy processed their credit card she waited for one last complaint.

'It was all right here.' Mrs J carefully covered the keypad as she put in her number. 'You've got some work to do, but I think you might see us again. Don't you, Ken?'

He nodded. She took her credit card slip, put it neatly into her wallet and turned on her heel, Ken following as ever. At the door he turned, grinned and gave Judy a thumbs-up sign.

Smiling she returned to the kitchen where Kelly was singing along to the radio as she and Mavis emptied the dishwasher.

'The Jacksons say they're coming back,' she announced.

'Oh, no!' they chorused.

Kelly swung her newly bobbed hair. 'If I'm lucky, I'll be away visiting Matt when they come.'

Judy looked thoughtful. When they came again Gordon would be home all the time.

Back at Reception, Mr Payne handed over his credit card.

'I hope you've enjoyed your stay?'

'Mmm.' He punched in his pin number and as he took back his card, he announced. 'I'm from the Tourist Board. I was here to inspect you.'

'What personally?' nerves made Judy flippant.

'No,' he said seriously, 'the hotel. I think we'd better sit down for a chat.'

She took him through to the lounge as Mavis, triumphant, busied herself in the breakfast room.

Two hours later, Judy felt as though she'd been through the mill. Mr Payne had been very thorough, but fair. 'Just one other thing,' he said as he left, 'I'm really impressed with your pastoral care of your staff. There's a very nice atmosphere around this place.'

Judy breathed a sigh of relief. She could even cope with Mavis crowing about being right with an accolade like that.

By the following Wednesday Judy knew she was driving everyone mad. She couldn't settle to anything and was biting people's heads off for no good reason. As she dusted her own quarters for the tenth time she reasoned with herself that she was being silly. Gordon had come and gone throughout their marriage. She was used to it, had even grown to enjoy her own time and, of course, the reunions, so why was she so nervous this time?

Peter found her polishing the cheese plant. 'Got time to talk?'

She grinned. 'Yes, hair appointment and manicure this afternoon, otherwise I'm all yours.'

Peter gazed at her appraisingly. 'Well, you know what I think. Don't change a thing!' Abruptly he looked away. 'I've had more responses to the internet dating site. After my experience with Moira, I think perhaps I need some guidance.'

Judy giggled. 'I'll make time for that.' Moira had seemed like a nice genteel lady in her profile, but had turned out to be something of a man-eater and Peter felt he was lucky to escape unscathed after she'd pinned him against the car at the end of the evening. It had made him wary.

Lucy arrived to find Peter, Mavis and Judy clustered round the computer in hysterics over some of the profiles people had put on the internet.

'Look at this,' Mavis cried, 'this one says she's fifty but look at the picture. That woman's seventy if she's a day.'

'And,' added Judy, 'she claims to be a natural blonde, but that's out of a bottle.'

Bosun was the first to notice Lucy and he launched himself at her with gleeful yaps.

'Sorry, the door was open.'

'Hello darling, the doors are open all the time to try and get some air moving. The heat!' Judy leapt from her chair to greet her daughter with a big hug. 'Nervous?'

'No. Just fraught. There's so much I've organised that has to come together. When's Dad home?'

'Comes into Heathrow at ten o'clock tomorrow morning. He's catching the coach to Bournemouth and I'm meeting him there.'

'What? You're not going to the airport? You always meet him.'

'I've got breakfasts,' Judy reminded her gently. 'There's no one else to cook and, even if there was, Kelly's off saying good bye to Matt, so I'm short staffed.'

'Oh,' Lucy oozed disapproval. Judy chose to ignore it. 'Anyway, Mum. I've got a great list of stuff to talk to you about and then we need to go and see the caterers, the florist and the hairdresser.'

'Um,' Judy struggled to sound understanding. 'Why do we have to do all of that? They're all sorted out.'

'Yes, but I can't just leave it at that. I've had some ideas about the greenery for the bouquets and I need to check the vol-au-vent fillings, oh and I've brought down my hair accessories for Nicola to decide how she's going to use them. By the way, Mum, what are you going to be wearing the night before the wedding? As the photographer's coming to do some casual shots, I want to be sure that we complement each other.'

'Um, jeans and whatever shirt is clean at the time?'

Lucy stared at her. 'Tell me you're joking.'

Judy longed to wind up her daughter, but she also knew that she'd be buying trouble for the future. 'Yes, I'm joking.' She considered. 'Well, sort of. I mean, I'll wear whatever you ask, so long as I have it. But honestly, Lucy don't you think you're going over the top. It's all organised, it'll be fine.'

'Well,' said Lucy, crisply, 'it will so long as I keep on top of it all. By the way, have you heard from Tom? He told Jason he'd hire his own tails, but I haven't heard that he's actually done it.'

'Lucy, he's doing exams. You try talking to him about anything this week and he'll bite your head off. He'll sort it out.'

'Hmm.' Lucy looked unconvinced. 'Well, I'll pop in later before I head back to London. I can see you're busy,' she looked pointedly at Peter. 'I'm off to check the florist has somewhere to keep the lilies chilled, and to see Nicola about hair.'

She turned at the door, 'By the way, I had a long leisurely lunch with Granny the other day. She wanted to hear all about the arrangements.' And she was gone.

Judy winced.

'I imagine,' said Peter slowly, 'that this is what it feels like after a hurricane.'

Judy signed. 'She's just overwrought. It'll all be over in a couple of weeks.'

Judy was up at six the next morning. She knew she wouldn't be able to go back to sleep so she got up, quietly put Bosun on his lead and let herself out of the house for a walk along the beach before her guests rose.

As she walked in the cool dawn, it occurred to her that she wouldn't be able to please herself so easily from now on. She'd be part of a couple again. There was always this mix of fear and anticipation before Gordon came home – worry that they might not be able to settle together again and excitement at seeing the man she loved more than anyone else in the world. This time, though, was different. So much had changed in the months he'd been away.

She had new friends and a life he knew little about. He hadn't even met Mavis and Kelly who were the total mainstays of life at White Oaks – so many people he didn't know. She thought of Sandhaven as home, but it felt like her home rather than theirs. There was a lot of catching up to do.

Reluctantly she called Bosun and turned back.

She'd done all she could. She'd engineered it so that she had few guests in tonight so they could go out. A table was booked at The Stockpot, the best restaurant in town and she planned to take him to The Anchor for a drink first.

Tomorrow, she had guests coming in for a christening so she'd be busy and then it was all go in preparation for Lucy and Jason's wedding the following weekend. Just for today, though, she was free to devote herself to Gordon and try to work out exactly how he'd fit into life at White Oaks.

The phone was ringing as she walked into the house. She glanced at her watch. It was before seven. It had to be family.

'Darling?'

'Gordon! You're supposed to be in the air!'

'We're fog-bound.' Her heart sank. She was so keyed up; everything had been geared towards today.

'Oh, no. So, when?'

'Same flight, but tomorrow. I'll be in at Heathrow at ten and then I'll get the coach to Bournemouth. Can you pick me up?'

Mentally, she re-arranged her day. 'Of course. But how disappointing and tomorrow…' she was about to launch into an explanation of why she'd be busy tomorrow and how she'd cleared today but he was briskly efficient.

'Right, see you then. Can't wait. Love you!' And he was gone.

Slowly she put the phone down. 'You too,' she murmured in the silence.

The coach drew into the bay at the Bus Station in Bournemouth and Judy realised she was holding her breath. It was hot and she'd looked her best when she left home, but after a half-hour drive and waiting in the sun she felt sticky and bedraggled. Her hair was damp and she was sure her make-up had run.

Gordon stepped down from the coach and all her doubts disappeared. He searched for her, she ran towards him and as his arms went round her she was once again the eighteen year old girl who'd fallen in love with her handsome sailor.

He released her and looked down. 'You look great!'

She laughed, 'I doubt it.'

'You do! You look different. Can't put my finger on it.'

She took his spare hand which wasn't lugging a large suitcase. 'Come on, let's go home.'

They chatted easily on the way home. As she drove, Judy tried to bring him up to speed on all that had gone on, but she kept having to stop to answer questions.

'Who are Matt and Josh?'

'Oh, Matt's Kelly's boyfriend. He's off to the Red Sea so she's a bit down in the dumps but Josh is back from Uni so he'll cheer her up and he's brilliant as a chamber-maid or room attendant, as he likes to call it. I did email you about him.'

'I'm sure you did, but it all became a bit of a blur.' He paused. 'When you don't know the people it seems a bit distant and irrelevant,' he admitted.

'Well it would,' she reasoned. 'You'll soon be in the swing of it.'

'I guess I'd better get on and decorate the bridal suite ready for Lucy and the idiot.'

'Oh, that's all done. Jim's been a godsend and Josh's mates gave us a headstart on that. And, actually, I've got tell you – Jason's not so bad when you get to know him properly. He's really been quite helpful. He and Tom washed the whole kitchen down after the fire.'

'Fire?' He looked horrified and belatedly she remembered she'd thought it best not to mention the grill fire.

'Oh, nothing serious.'

As Judy drove into Sandhaven, looking its very best in the June sun, Gordon sighed. 'I'm so glad I don't have to go back to sea. This is going to be so good, Jude.'

'It's good already,' she reminded him. 'It's just going to be better now you're home.'

Proudly, Judy took Gordon on a tour of inspection. She was delighted with his reaction. The rooms were clean and bright and all had little personal touches, flowers and pictures.

'You've done a fantastic job, Jude. The

place looks completely different.'

Back in the privacy of their own quarters, Gordon took her in his arms. 'I'm sorry I wasn't here for all this.' He nuzzled her ear. 'Have I told you how much I love you?'

Judy leant into him, thrilled he was back and that she had someone to share it all with. His hands moved over her body and she melted, realising how much she'd missed him.

Then the bell went.

Judy groaned. 'Get used to it,' she murmured. 'It always happens at the wrong moment.'

'I'll go.' Gordon volunteered.

'Hello, we're Mr and Mrs Mumford.'

'Oh, yes. You're for the Christening, are you? Er, you fill in the registration form and I'll see what room you're in.'

He went out the back. 'There's a list on the desk,' said Judy, 'and you need to tell them what time breakfast is, that the bar will be open, that they can't smoke and…'

'You do it. I don't even know the answers to some of those.'

Judy went to greet the guests and led them upstairs, giving the usual litany of check-in information as she went. As soon as the Mumfords were settled, the next set of guests arrived and it was half an hour before she returned to the sitting room to find Gordon sitting in the chair reading the paper with Bosun settled, blissfully, on his knee.

He looked up, embarrassed. 'I think I need a training course.'

'Just listen and learn.'

The bell went again and Judy left the door ajar while she checked in one set of guests while explaining to another where the church was and giving a third some suggestions of places to eat.

'You don't need me.'

'I need you more than ever before,' she said honestly, her heart breaking at how lost he looked, 'but you're going to have to do things my way. I know what works.'

At that moment, the door to Reception opened and Mavis appeared.

'Ah,' she looked Gordon up and down, 'the wanderer returns. I'm Mavis, I'm sure you've heard about me.'

'Of course.'

'I hope you appreciate all your wife's done. I've never known anyone work so hard.'

'Believe me, I can see the difference.' Judy watched Gordon turn on the charm, knowing that it would cut no ice with Mavis.

'You've obviously been a great help too.'

'I've only done my job. I've taken my orders from the Boss here,' she indicated Judy and turned to talk to her, ignoring Gordon completely. 'I came in because I forgot to tell you where I'd put the post this morning.'

Judy smiled. She knew Mavis couldn't wait till tomorrow to see what Gordon was like.

Mavis went to the kitchen and re-emerged with a pile of letters. 'I remembered putting it in with the table cloths,' she explained handing them to Judy.

Judy opened a letter from the Tourist Board. 'Hey,' she turned to Mavis, 'we got a Three Diamond rating. Mr Payne came up with the goods!'

'Mr Payne?' Gordon was struggling to catch up again.

'The Inspector. And he was a pain! That was the day Kelly found out about Matt going away and the Jacksons…' Judy began and then stopped, realising that Gordon hadn't a clue what she was talking about. The phone rang in Judy's pocket.

'White Oaks Guest House. Oh, hello Lucy. Dad's home! Shall I pass you over?'

There was a howl from the other end.

'What? No, now come on. Lucy, calm down! What's the matter?'

'Tell me she doesn't want to marry that idiot,' murmured Gordon and Judy glared at him.

'Lucy,' Judy spoke sharply. 'Get real! We can find another photographer. It's not the end of the world. Don't be so silly, of course we don't have to cancel the wedding. I'll call you back.' She put the phone down and turned to Mavis.

'Eleanor!' They cried in unison.

'I'll 'phone her now,' said Mavis.

Judy turned to Gordon. 'Eleanor Samuels did our brochures,' she began but Mavis interrupted. 'I'll get her number, it's in my bag. She'll be so pleased.'

Judy saw it coming before the accident happened. Mavis, on a mission, didn't see Gordon's suitcase and fell over it hitting the ground with a huge thump.

Judy and Gordon rushed to her aid as she gripped her leg, which was out at a most peculiar angle.

'Oh, my God. Gordon, quick, call an ambulance. That leg's obviously broken.'

Mavis groaned and Judy detected a glint of a tear. Its obviously hurt a lot. 'Give me the phone,' said Mavis weakly, 'and I'll phone Eleanor about the photographs.'

The photographs, thought Judy, were the least of her problems. She was going to have to do this whole wedding without Mavis. That thought was truly terrifying.

Ten

Happy Ever After

Judy was hiding in the larder. If someone had produced a spaceship and offered her a trip to Mars she'd have jumped at the chance to escape White Oaks Guest House. She knew she couldn't stay there long, but her little oasis of peace among the cornflakes seemed like the last bastion of sanity in the whole place.

She sighed, straightened her shoulders as though preparing for battle, and entered the fray.

Gordon was just extricating the third suitcase from the back of his in-laws' car and Judy had to admire his restraint. Her parents hadn't been expected till this evening but in the middle of breakfast they had wandered into the kitchen.

'Darling!' Her mother air-kissed Judy, who was just placing two poached eggs onto a slice of brown toast. 'Do you suppose someone could bring the luggage in for us?'

'Later. We're a seaside bed and breakfast, not the Savoy. I don't have flunkies standing about doing nothing.' Judy knew she'd snapped unfairly but her mother always brought out the worst in her.

'It's all right, I'll do it. Come on, Rose.' Gordon had ushered her out of the kitchen, glad, Judy thought, to have something to do. Slotting Gordon into the business was proving difficult.

Wedding fever had gripped White Oaks. Judy had called her daughter's marriage the Wedding of the Year, but Mavis had countered quite rightly that it was more like the Wedding of a Lifetime.

Everyone was going out of their way to make sure that Lucy's day was exactly as she wanted it. When the upmarket photographer, chosen by Lucy, had been summoned to The Maldives for the nuptials of a well-known rock star, Eleanor Samuels had come to the rescue.

'The Sandhaven Magic', Mavis had dubbed Eleanor's renaissance, but Eleanor had put it all down to Judy, Mavis and the friendly relaxing atmosphere of White Oaks.

Lucy had faxed a list of all the pre-wedding shots she wanted and Eleanor had simply smiled. 'The client is always right,' she'd murmured as she'd gone off to picture the outside of the hair dressing salon that Lucy was using.

Bosun was going into kennels against Gordon's wishes.

'He's my dog and he's part of the family,' he'd argued, but Judy had reminded him that her mother would be there along with the caterers and people coming in and out of their own accommodation.

'We just can't risk him leaving home again,' she'd insisted and, grudgingly, he'd conceded the point.

It worried Judy that Gordon was having to do a lot of giving in. Once the wedding was out of the way, they were going to have to address seriously how they were going to split the work. Now that Gordon was home full-time he needed a job, but for now it was all hands to the deck.

'When's the bride arriving?' Rose asked.

'Lunchtime.'

'Oh, good. Perhaps we can all go out for lunch?'

'I can't,' said Judy shortly, 'I've too much to do here but if you'd like to take Lucy and Jason out that might be a good idea. Keep them out of my hair!'

'I'll see what she says when she gets here.

I don't suppose there's a chance of a cup of coffee?'

Mavis appeared. Although she was on crutches, she'd insisted on coming into work, unpaid, to supervise and help out where she could. Judy was well aware that in reality she just couldn't bear to be left out. 'There's still some in the pot in the dining room,' she said, waving a crutch in that direction, 'but you'll have to wash your own mug. Kitchen's all cleaned.'

Peter wandered into the hall without knocking and Gordon bristled. Judy had foreseen this problem but could do nothing about it. Judy was not going to ban him just because Gordon was behaving like a territorial rottweiler.

'Peter,' she kissed him lightly on the cheek, 'welcome to Chaosville.'

''Scuse me.' Gordon pushed past him with a suitcase and headed upstairs.

Peter turned to Rose and Geoffrey. 'I saw the car and wondered if you'd like to come round to my place for a peaceful cup of coffee? It's a bit hectic here.'

Rose looked doubtful. 'Well, we came early to be helpful, but...'

'Actually,' Geoffrey looked at his daughter's face and stepped in quickly. 'After the drive a nice cuppa would be lovely. Thank you, Peter.' He turned to Judy. 'That all right with you, love? Be back in an hour or so.'

'Fine,' she murmured weakly and they all went off chatting brightly about the forecast for tomorrow which, mercifully, was for a hot sunny day. Judy was fairly sure that God would not have dared give her daughter anything less for her wedding.

'If anyone else wants coffee, send 'em round,' said Peter as he shepherded Geoffrey and Rose out of White Oaks.

With her parents safely out of the way, last night's guests checked out and the wedding party not arriving for a couple of hours, Judy thought it sensible to review everything to make sure that nothing had been missed in the preparations for the big day tomorrow. Jan and Martin were bringing the cake, which was being made by an old neighbour from The Close, but they weren't coming till tomorrow, the morning of the wedding.

'I wish Jan was coming today. It'd be comforting to have the cake here. One less thing to worry about.'

'Honestly, Jude.' Gordon demurred, 'you're treating this like some sort of military campaign. In the end, it's two people getting married. That's all.'

Mavis nearly choked on her coffee. 'You can tell you haven't been around for the last few months,' she said dryly.

Judy's mobile bleeped in her pocket heralding a text. She reached for it with trepidation. If it was Lucy it would be a panic and she couldn't handle a crisis now. Tom, on the other hand, had breezily stayed distant from the wedding plans. He'd assured his sister that he'd turn up, wearing tails and on time but beyond that he refused to be involved. Judy envied him his detachment.

'On the way. With you soon. Tell Luce bringing Siobhan. C u later. T xxx'

'Well, what is it now?' Gordon had clearly had enough already.

'Tom He's on his way, but he's bringing this new girlfriend.'

Mavis grinned. She had a huge soft spot for Judy's son who treated her like a slightly batty aunt. 'Lucy'll love that. An extra uninvited guest. How will she cope?'

'She'll kill him. Actually, it is naughty. He can't just go around inviting people to his sister's wedding.'

'Who's the girl?' Mavis asked, absent-mindedly polishing a spoon on her jumper.

‘She’s a fellow student, though I think she might be a year or two older. She’s doing Design and he’s obviously smitten. He rang me up at midnight after their first date to tell me all about her.’

‘Well, we should be pleased he’s bringing her home.’ Gordon rose and stretched. ‘I’m going to take Bosun to the kennels. Under pressure.’ He added.

‘You will be back when Lucy and Jason get here, won’t you?’

He didn’t answer but picked up the little terrier and grinned naughtily over his shoulder as he left.

Eleanor passed him in the doorway. ‘Right, I think I’m on schedule.’ She consulted a piece of dog-eared paper. ‘Yes, I’ve done what I can.’

‘My parents are round at Peter’s next door, having coffee. Why don’t you go and join them?’ Judy smiled. Eleanor was one of her favourite people.

‘Are you sure?’ Eleanor looked doubtful and Judy marvelled at the change in the woman. In black jeans and tee-shirt and sporting a new highlighted spiky haircut she was clearly beginning to enjoy life again and looked every inch the professional photographer.

'Yes. He said it was open house and it's less chaotic than here.'

'Okay, then. See you in a bit. I'll take the camera. The list says "Candid shots of relatives" so I can snap your parents.'

'Make sure Mum's got all the war paint on then. She'll be miffed if she doesn't think she looks her absolute best.'

Lucy and Jason arrived on the dot of twelve – a whirlwind of brisk efficiency.

'Thought this was supposed to be romantic?' murmured Judy as Lucy set up her laptop to call up her 'wedding schedule'.

'That's tomorrow.' She had the grace to laugh. 'Now why is Granddad's car outside?'

'They arrived hours ago. They've had coffee with Peter and now they're upstairs waiting for you to get here. They'd like to take you out to lunch.'

'Like I've got time for that!' Lucy raised her eyes heavenwards and Judy gave her a motherly look. 'Yes, okay. I know. She has bought me the most wonderful dress.'

'Which I've yet to see,' reminded her mother.

Lucy gave a mysterious smile. 'Wait till tomorrow. I think you'll be impressed.' She turned to Jason. 'Come on then, let's go and brave the grandparents and we can all go out for a sandwich. I daren't eat much or the dress won't do up.' They disappeared upstairs just as the front door opened and Tom walked in followed by one of the most beautiful girls Judy had ever seen.

Tom was doing his best to hide a smirk that Judy recognised. It was the same grin he'd worn when, against all the odds, he'd come out with four straight A's at A'level.

'Hi Mum.' Ultra-casual, ultra-cool.

'Tom!' She gave him a big hug and smiled at the girl with him. She had long auburn hair, apparently curling naturally over her shoulders, though Judy suspected it was artfully arranged to look casual.

'Mum, this is Siobhan.'

'I thought it might be. Lovely to meet you.' Judy couldn't decide whether to kiss her or shake hands. The girl made it easy by leaning forward and pecking her on the cheek.

In a classy and charming Irish brogue, she apologised. 'I feel awful gate-crashing your wedding like this. Tom said it would be all right, but I'd hate it if someone did it to me.'

'It's fine with me.' Judy liked her already. 'It's his sister you have to negotiate with.'

Tom took Siobhan's hand. 'If Lucy wants me, particularly dressed up like a penguin, she gets you. I wasn't going to leave you behind,' he added softly.

Judy looked away in the face of such obvious emotion. What a shame Lucy and Jason didn't behave like this. For a split second she wondered if Gordon was right and she should have put up more obstacles to this marriage. Firmly, she put the thought aside. Too late.

Lucy came down the stairs and greeted Tom with a sisterly push.

'Hi Bro.' She completely ignored Siobhan, presuming, no doubt, that she was 'hired help' of some sort. 'Got your suit?'

'Whoops! I knew there was something. I've been so busy… I've got clean jeans.'

Lucy took a deep breath. 'Tom, you promised, you can't do this.' Judy giggled silently, she knew a wind-up when she saw one.

Siobhan stepped in. 'It's okay. He's got a fabulous suit and,' she looked at him and smiled, 'he looks a dream in it.'

Lucy gave him a shove. 'Don't torment me today,' she warned. She turned to Siobhan. 'And you are?'

Tom intervened. 'This is Siobhan, she's with me. We're together,' he added unnecessarily.

Siobhan kissed Lucy. 'Congratulations on your wedding, and, listen, don't mind him. I understand about tomorrow. If numbers are a problem I'll take myself off for the day. I don't want to intrude.'

In the face of such Gaelic charm, even Lucy crumbled. 'Don't be daft,' she smiled, 'it'll be good to have you there. Tom needs someone to keep him in order.'

'Well, thanks then. I'm looking forward to it.'

Lucy turned to her brother. 'You'd better come and see the grandparents. They're holed up in their bedroom keeping out of the way. You too,' she added over her shoulder to Siobhan.

The day passed in a flurry of activity and it was six o'clock before they all gathered in the tiny bar for a drink. Gordon was ensconced behind the counter where he seemed most at home and the rest of the family was drifting in for pre-dinner drinks.

Judy had booked a table at The Anchor where Sharon had promised champagne on the house before the meal. This dinner was for family only and Mavis was staying home to show in Lucy and Jason's friends who were coming down after work. Quite how she was going to do this when she couldn't do stairs was beyond Judy, but it was a problem, like several others, she'd just decided to ignore.

Siobhan in jeans and white shirt and looking a million dollars offered to stay in with Mavis and help. 'I'm not going to gate-crash dinner too.' Tom tried to argue, but she insisted. 'I'm not family. I'll stay here.'

Mavis, propped up in the corner with a sweet sherry, looked pleased.

Always direct, she asked what others had wondered. 'So where did you meet young Tom then, love?'

Siobhan blushed prettily. 'I work in the Student Union Bar, Tom has a habit of being the last to leave.'

Gordon grinned. 'Chip off the old block, eh?'

The family banter continued and even Rose, who always failed to 'get' jokes until ten minutes after everyone else, joined in with the teasing.

Judy just hoped this spirit of co-operation could last another twenty-four hours. She watched Gordon as he poured Jason another pint and warned him against getting married with a hangover.

'I did that,' he commented and Judy remembered Gordon going out with his

Navy friends the night before their wedding, 'and it's really not a good idea.'

Tom slapped his brother-in-law-to-be on the back. 'I'm sure he's got written permission to have two pints. After that he has to check with the boss.'

'Um,' Jason pretended to consult a piece of paper, 'three pints and a whisky I'm allowed. Then I have to go back and get permission for more.'

'Which,' Lucy said tartly, but with a smile, 'will not be granted.'

They all laughed and Judy sat back with satisfaction watching her family enjoying themselves.

As Judy laid out croissants, bagels, fruit and yoghurts she wondered whether it would actually have been easier to do a normal cooked breakfast. The idea had been that this would be quicker and leave her more time for other things. Kelly would do tea and toast and Judy would not have to cook, but she thought she'd rather have stayed in her usual routine. Still, looking at Lucy's London friends she reasoned they must live on fruit and muesli anyway, she'd never seen so many stick-thin women.

A text arrived from Jan just as Judy was

warming another tray of croissants.

'Mum-in-law fallen. Coming a.s.a.p. Will be there! Love to all'.

Judy couldn't believe it. The one person she wanted with her on this particular day, who'd been through all the trials and tribulations of child-rearing with her, and she might not make it.

Suddenly she remembered the cake. Jan had the cake. The centrepiece of the dining room – three layers in colours to match the bride's bouquet – all perfectly planned and not here. Judy quashed the rising panic in her chest and decided the only answer was to keep quiet and hope Jan arrived before Lucy realised there was a problem.

The morning flew by. Lucy's friends came and went in a haze of Harvey Nichols hat-boxes; Gordon's sister, a farmer's wife from Devon, arrived with tales of woe about milk yields and announced she wasn't staying for the Reception and then, in amongst the chaos, came another text from Jan.

'Leaving in an hour.'

Judy looked at her watch. Time was going to be very tight.

Mavis came upon her staring vacantly at a pile of towels. 'Why so glum?'

She explained. Mavis patted her on the

shoulder awkwardly. 'You've got lots of friends here, you know,' she assured her and Judy marvelled again that she'd found such good staff in Sandhaven. Everyone was pitching in. Kelly had cleared breakfast single-handed and now she and Mavis were to re-arrange the dining room ready for the florist and the caterers.

'It's not just Jan, it's the cake. She's got the damned cake!'

'That's okay,' said Kelly, taking the towels from her, 'we'll lock the dining room door and tell Lucy the caterers don't want to be disturbed. She won't realise it's not in there.'

Judy wasn't sure that would work, but it was the best option so she nodded gratefully and went to check on the drinks.

Josh, who'd fortunately finished Uni the day before, had been commandeered by Gordon and they were busy with glasses, champagne and other alcohol-related tasks. They were all busy and nobody was complaining about the work.

At twelve-thirty, Judy had to be at the hairdresser and she knew that by then everything needed to be ready so at midday she walked right round the hotel, checking everything. Her parents were in a first floor room with a bay window and as she knocked on their door she found them sitting looking at the view, enjoying the peace.

'This is a lovely room, darling. Lucy and Jason should have it.'

'They're not staying tonight. They're going to The Limes Hotel for a bit of real luxury and, of course, last night Lucy only needed a single. Jason stayed down the road so they wouldn't meet this morning.'

'Nice that they've taken all the traditions on board, isn't it?' said Rose.

'It's odd that they bother when they live together anyway,' Geoffrey commented.

'Well, you know what I think about that,' said Rose briskly, 'but then I'm just old-fashioned.' She waited for someone to contradict her but there was an unsettling pause.

'Anyway,' said Judy brightly. 'There's sandwiches next door at Peter's if you want a bit of lunch, and the car is coming for us at two.'

'Couldn't we have lunch here?' Rose asked. 'It seems such an imposition on Peter.'

'It's fine. Mavis made the sandwiches last night and we took them round this morning. It leaves the kitchen and dining room here clear for the caterers. Anyway,' time to change the subject, 'I must get to the hair-dressers.'

She went on round the building, delighting at how it all looked. All the trauma and hard work had paid off, bookings were good for July and August and Judy was confident that she now had the basis of a successful business. She met Gordon on the stairs as she came back down.

'It looks nice, doesn't it?' she couldn't help asking, fishing, she knew, for a compliment.

'It does. Left me a bit high and dry, though, hasn't it. I don't know what I'm going to do, you know. You don't need me.' He pulled a letter from his pocket. 'This came this morning, confirming the end of my contract at sea. So, here I am, redundant and ready for action.'

'Hey!' She hugged him. 'It's what we wanted. It'll be fine.'

The doorbell rang and Judy ran to answer it. What seemed like an army of caterers marched in, laden with Tupperware boxes, glass bowls and huge platters. They were a very professional bunch and Judy found them scarily efficient. She'd promised them two waiting staff and she felt fiercely protective as she introduced Kelly and Josh. Stella, the supervisor, looked them up and down and gave a curt nod. Presumably they'd passed muster. The florists had been and gone and there were huge flower arrangements all around the dining room. Judy, locking the door so that Lucy couldn't notice the conspicuously empty centre table, hardly recognised the place. It looked stunning; she was just pleased that Lucy and Jason were paying for their own wedding – the whole thing must be costing a fortune.

Gathered in the hall, Judy thought what an elegant crowd they made. Her navy suit, trimmed with pink piping, struck just the right note and she was pleased that one of Lucy's friends, who might have been called Melissa, had complimented her on it. Tom had gone off to meet Jason, resplendent in a wonderful suit and a beautiful gold waistcoat which was obviously a tribute to Siobhan's immaculate taste. Siobhan herself wore dark green silk which set her hair off perfectly.

Kelly and Josh, smart in black and white ready to work after the ceremony, stood slightly to one side, stifling giggles as Mavis made her entrance.

'Have you checked the sitting room sofa?' Kelly murmured in Judy's ear, 'looks like Mavis has borrowed the covers.' Mavis' ample bosom was draped, rather too tightly, in huge pink roses on a riotously coloured background. She'd certainly stand out.

'Nice dress, Mavis,' Judy knew she was expected to comment.

'Bought it for my niece's wedding in 1988. Haven't had much of a chance to wear it.'

Gradually everyone dispersed for the short walk to the Church. Siobhan had thoughtfully ordered a taxi for Mavis and went with her to keep her company.

Eventually there was only Gordon, Judy and her parents in the hall. Judy had tried not to feel left out as she'd been banned from Lucy's room during the preparations. Rose, however, had been allowed in. Judy realised this was fair since Lucy's granny had stumped up for the dress but she still felt that Lucy was paying her back for her initial lack of enthusiasm about the wedding.

All that was put behind them, however, as Lucy appeared on the stairs. Judy gasped. How could this vision possibly be her daughter?

The Vera Wang dress certainly lived up to expectations and more. Judy had thought the extravagance over-the-top, but Lucy looked absolutely stunning. Her slim figure was corseted into a beautifully-cut ivory silk dress shimmering with thousands of hand-sewn beads. It was very simple and unbelievably effective. She began her stately descent while the friend who was bridesmaid arranged a long fishtail train behind her as she walked. Gordon, tears in his eyes, stepped forward and held out his arm and together they stood for Eleanor who was discreetly snapping the family group.

Judy turned to Rose and hugged her. 'Thanks for doing this for her, Mum, she looks wonderful.'

She approached Lucy who squealed and held up her bouquet in defence. 'Don't! You'll squash me,' she laughed.

'Okay, but I have got to say, you look…' she was lost for words, 'amazing!'

The ceremony passed in a blur. As Lucy promised to love and honour Jason, Judy saw Tom turn and search for Siobhan seated a few pews back with Kelly, Mavis and Peter. She'd have to start worrying about him now. He was so young, hadn't even finished Uni, and he'd fallen hook, line and sinker for a girl who was perfect for him – just not yet. Still, Judy knew that all she could do now was love her children and be there for them. The future belonged to her and Gordon.

She sighed. Gordon felt for her hand and smiled down at her.

They posed on the church steps for a few pictures but Lucy and Jason had decided that the main photographs should be taken in the garden at White Oaks. Judy had set Gordon to the task of making sure it was up to the mark and he'd spent a fortune on bedding plants for instant colour.

A car had been arranged to take Judy's parents back to the guest house, but everyone else was to walk.

Just before the ceremony, Judy had caught her mother. 'Mavis is going to go back with you, I've just realised she can't walk back and I haven't arranged anything for her.'

Rose had raised her eyebrows. 'But she's not, well, you know, family.'

Judy cared not a jot. 'You have a car with a spare seat in it, she's on crutches. She comes with you.'

Her father, as usual, had seen sense. 'That's fine. I'll keep an eye out for her at the end of the service.'

The wedding party assembled for the walk back to White Oaks. Led by Lucy and Jason they strolled along the seafront. Tourists stopped and watched, all smiles; people came out from the shops and Judy waved as

Sharon ran out of the Anchor to give Lucy a lucky horseshoe.

There was a flurry of excitement as a flare went up from the lifeboat station. It exploded into the sky with a huge bang and for a moment it seemed as though it was part of the celebrations until the lifeboat shot out from its boathouse and sped across bay.

Gordon turned to her. 'I've been thinking. I might volunteer for the lifeboat. It'd mean some training, but I know boats and it would help me meet people. Reckon I'd be good at that.'

Judy was surprised to find how relieved she felt. Gordon's lack of a role had really been niggling at her. She took his hand. 'I'd still be around for most of the time, but it would be another string to my bow. Might even buy a boat and do trips in the bay next summer.'

'Great idea.' She was thrilled that he sounded so positive but she just had to add one caveat. 'Aren't you too old?'

He grinned. 'No, not on the scrapheap yet. I can volunteer till I'm fifty five so I've got plenty of good years left in me. Well, eight anyway!'

They strolled along chatting to the other guests who were uniformly spellbound by the beauty of Sandhaven Bay. Boats bobbed at anchor and the white cliffs of the Isle of Wight in the distance were like a painted backdrop.

'It's like something off a nineteen-fifties postcard,' said Ayesha, a colleague of Jason's, and her friend agreed.

'And people are so friendly. I went into the chemist this morning and everyone in there knew I was down for the wedding before I even spoke.'

'They would,' agreed Judy, waving at the girls from the hairdresser who'd all come out to watch.

The wedding car glided by and Mavis waved graciously, rather like the Queen Mother draped in a curtain.

As they arrived back at White Oaks, Kelly and Josh were standing in the front garden with trays of champagne.

Kelly proffered her tray. 'Would Madam like a drink?' she enquired of Judy.

'Madam thinks she should stick to orange juice for a while. Better stay sober.'

'Nonsense,' Gordon took a glass for her. 'You've done all the hard work, it'll run itself now.'

'We'll make sure everything's all right,'

Kelly insisted. 'Go on!'

Judy laughed, wondering if relying solely on Kelly to ensure the smooth running of Lucy's wedding, was really a good idea. 'Oh, all right then.'

Lucy came up. 'Right, Mum, Dad. Photo time. Eleanor thinks it would be best if we all spread over the steps. In his role as Best Man, Tom's supposed to be helping her as he knows who everyone is, but he seems to be otherwise engaged.'

They all looked across to where Tom was deep in conversation with Siobhan. As they watched he idly played with a strand of her hair and stroked her wrist.

'I think he's busy,' said Gordon with masterly understatement. 'I'll do it.'

'You can't,' Lucy pointed out. 'You'll be in the pictures.'

Eleanor was setting up a tripod. 'Tom's been side-tracked, so Peter's going to help me.' Peter came and joined the group. 'Right, let's get you working.' She consulted her list. 'Bride, groom and bride's parents.'

Peter laughed. 'Well, that's an easy one.' He chivvied Judy and Gordon towards the steps and reached into the pocket of Eleanor's jacket for her list. Judy thought it a very intimate gesture. 'I'll set up the next lot,' he said.

'Thanks,' Eleanor said absently, looking through her viewfinder and composing the shot.

'No problem,' he touched her shoulder briefly as he left and Mavis sidled up to Judy.

'Another couple in the making, I reckon.'

'Yes,' Judy agreed, 'and I didn't even see it coming.'

'Neither did Eleanor till yesterday. But they're good together, aren't they?' Mavis was uncharacteristically dewy-eyed.

'Yes,' said Judy, thoughtfully, 'they are.' Both lonely with a lot to offer and two of the nicest people you could ever meet. Perfect!

In her handbag, her mobile chirruped. She reached for it automatically. 'White Oaks Guest House,' she announced. Mavis, Eleanor and Gordon looked at her in amazement.

'The end of July? No, I'm sorry I've nothing left for that weekend. Hope we can help another time.'

Lucy took the phone from her and threw it to Tom, who caught it deftly. 'You are not taking bookings during my wedding, Mother.' She looked around. 'Siobhan, will you look after that and tell anyone who rings to call back tomorrow.'

'Sure,' Siobhan grinned.

'But I need the business,' Judy began.

'Not today you don't!' They chorused and she laughed.

For the next few minutes Eleanor was busy taking photographs while Peter co-ordinated the guests. They made a great team and it was a slick operation.

'One last formal photograph,' Eleanor consulted her list. The guests were all milling about the garden. Somehow, Judy felt Lucy had managed to pull off a formal wedding with the atmosphere of an upmarket Garden Party. Everyone was mixing and chatting; out of the corner of her eye she could see Gordon listening intently to the vicar, while her mother was entrancing some of the young women with a tale from her youth.

Peter touched her on the arm. 'You and Gordon, on the steps of the hotel.'

Judy, on her second glass of champagne, had finally decided to relinquish all responsibility and just enjoy the day. She looked up at the building she'd grown to love. It had fought her all the way, but now she was so proud of White Oaks.

Gordon joined her on the steps and Eleanor took her picture.

Judy had an idea. 'Hang on! While you've got the camera there, Eleanor, can you do one more?'

She called her staff, 'Mavis, Kelly, Josh – come up here and join us.' Peter and Geoffrey quickly relieved Josh and Kelly of their trays and the White Oaks team gathered on the steps, Mavis somehow managing to stand between Judy and Gordon.

As they posed, Tom called everyone to order.

'Before we all go inside, although this day belongs to the happy couple, Lucy and I would just like to congratulate Mum and Dad, well, Mum particularly, on the transformation they've made to White Oaks.' There was a screech of brakes and a taxi drew to a halt. Jan jumped out and joined the edge of the crowd.

Discreetly, Siobhan slipped away and took three white boxes from the taxi driver, disappearing inside with them. Jan gave Judy a thumbs-up sign as Tom continued. 'Most of you haven't seen it until now, but the work they've put in has been just awesome and the result is stunning. Raise your glasses, folks, to White Oaks Guest House.'

The guests all toasted Judy, Gordon and the hotel and Judy burned with a fierce pride in White Oaks. They'd come a long way together.

Gordon looked across at her, over Mavis' head, and raised his glass. 'To us – and a future together,' he whispered and they clinked glasses as the staff dispersed.

Jan came over and hugged her. 'Martin's at the hospital with his Mum. I just couldn't miss this. And anyway…'

'The cake,' interrupted Judy. 'Shh! Lucy never realised it wasn't here.'

'Whoops,' they giggled together and it was just like old times.

Jan put an arm round her. 'Are you okay?'

Judy thought about it for a moment. 'Yes, I am. I really am!'

She left the crowd and walked out into the road where she could get a proper look at the front of the building. The Edwardian house looked its best with the sun picking out the filigree wrought iron balcony and the beautifully dressed crowd mingling on the front lawn.

Peter and Eleanor were chatting to Tom and Siobhan; Mavis was deep in conversation with Judy's father while her mother could be heard trilling unnecessary instructions to the caterers.

A car passed and Jim, the decorator, parped his horn in greeting. She waved cheerfully.

Judy belonged in Sandhaven now. She and Gordon would be fine here. This was home.

The publishers hope that this book has given you enjoyable reading. Large Print Books are especially designed to be as easy to see and hold as possible. If you wish a complete list of our books please ask at your local library or write directly to:

Dales Large Print Books
Magna House, Long Preston,
Skipton, North Yorkshire.
BD23 4ND